DEADRIDGE DOLL

"Don't move. If you even fart I'll blast you full of lead!" Spur's arms were steady. His fingers teased the trigger of his revolver.

Hardwick raised his ivory right brow. "How can you kill me? I'm legally dead."

"You're standing right there!"

"Yes. They did hang Fancy Freddie Hardwick the day you left St. Louis. It was a drunken bastard my men found on the street. Strange as it might seem, the man looked quite a lot like me." The albino smiled.

"That must have broken his mother's heart," McCoy said.

"Back off, McCoy!" Hardwick said. "This isn't the time. You'll know when it is!"

SPUR #34

DEADRIDGE DOLL

Dirk Fletcher

LEISURE BOOKS NEW YORK CITY

A LEISURE BOOK®

March 2006

Published by

Dorchester Publishing Co., Inc.
200 Madison Avenue
New York, NY 10016

ISBN 0-8439-3064-0

Printed in the United States of America.

Visit us on the web at www.dorchesterpub.com.

DEADRIDGE DOLL

CHAPTER ONE

Spur McCoy ducked. Hot lead spun overhead and slammed into the tilting wall. The train's dining car bucked like a saddled, unbroken horse. Spur overturned a cherrywood table and peeled off two shots at the gunman.

The thin, greasy-skinned man had just barged into the car and demanded the passenger's money. McCoy had instantly reacted.

"Kill him!" an elderly woman, the only other passenger in the car, screamed.

"Hang on, lady!"

Situated at the far end of the dining car, Spur peered over the table's square edge. The man in black was reloading. I've got you now, McCoy thought.

He rose and took aim. "Throw down your weapon! It's all over!"

"Is it?" The black-haired man smiled beneath

his moustache. He threw down his weapon and pulled the emergency stop cord that was near the gilt ceiling. The train instantly responded.

The sudden jolt lurched Spur from his feet. His six-foot frame banged onto the floorboards. The woman screamed again.

Silverware flew through the air. Crystal candleholders smashed around him. The agonized sound of metal scraping against metal vibrated through the dining car. Spur struggled to his feet, trying to resist the bone-jarring forces that slammed him backward again and again behind the table.

"He's getting away!" the old woman shouted.

"Shit!"

A heavy chandelier crashed on the table and skidded to the floor.

"This is no time for profanity, sir!"

McCoy pulled himself up. The train car seemed to elongate, to stretch around them. The far door lay open. Through it, Spur saw the would-be thief working on the hitch that connected the cars.

"Damnit!"

He raced through the dining car, dodged fallen objects and fired. The black-moustached man bent over and threw a hand to his shoulder.

But it was already too late. As Spur lined up his next shot the pressure that had been tearing apart the dining car suddenly ceased. The train surged away from its last two cars, skidding forward on its brakes.

The gentle hill that they'd been ascending now took over, tugging at the dining car and the caboose that lay behind it. The great iron wheels slowed and reversed their motion. The dining car soon gained momentum as it slid backwards down the foothill in the middle of Arizona Territory.

Spur took another shot at the departing gunman and stared out the door. It was too far to jump across; he'd never reach the rest of the train. McCoy turned to the old woman and frowned.

"Well!" the well-fed grandmother said, fanning her face. "A lot of help you were!"

"Look, ma'am, we have big problems to worry about right now."

"The train's stopping!" She extended a dainty finger toward the departing machine.

"But we're not!" Spur stuck his head through a shattered window and looked around. The heated desert air blasted his face and threatened to tug off his Stetson. McCoy glanced back and groaned.

A second train chugged up the hill toward them.

On the same track!

He cursed again. "Hell! They must have messed up the switching back in Yuma!" He withdrew from the window and wiped his forehead.

"Such language, young man!"

Spur waved her off. "I mentioned a problem?"

The plump woman stood, clutching her fox purse. "I know that! The train's getting away!"

"Shut up and listen! There's another train behind us."

"Fine!" The grandmother beamed. "Then we'll be able to get back to town."

"Aren't you listening? It's coming right at us.
It doesn't look like it can stop in time."

The elderly woman widened her brown eyes.
"Mercy!"

Gravity pulled the runaway caboose and
dining car. It bounced as it rolled down the
foothill, veering dangerously on the track. Its
speed increased by the second.

"I expect you to save me," the woman said.
"I haven't lived to the age of sixty just to wind
up smashed between two of these infernal
contraptions!"

Spur smiled at her. The floorboards rippled
beneath his boots. "Will you jump?"

She lifted her chin. "Never. I'm a lady. And
ladies don't jump!"

McCoy grabbed the woman's hand. "I don't
think the train's gonna stop for us. We're gonna
be pressed like duck liver. Come on!"

"Wait a minute!"

He wrestled the plump, elderly woman to
the yawning door. The two lines of metal
blurred as they sped past.

"You're tetched in the head. We'll be killed,"
she said in an even voice.

"You're right. The caboose!"

He shuffled her out of the dining car. The
caboose's door was locked.

"No time for picks," McCoy muttered as he
shot just below the knob. The lock fell out. He
pushed open the door.

A drunken train attendant snored on the
floor. Spur led the woman past him and flung
open the back door. The second train had
slowed as its engine dug into the grade. Spur
saw the rush of its air brakes.

"What can we do?" the woman said.

Spur poured the contents of a half finished bottle of whiskey onto the attendant's face. He spluttered and sat. "I *am* working, Mr. Taggert!" he instantly said, rubbing his eyes.

"No, you're not. We've got a runaway caboose here."

The youth winced. "Oh boy."

"*We* can jump," McCoy said. "Know any way we can get the old lady out in one piece?"

The red-eyed youth stood and looked around. "Damn! Let me think!" He pulled his wild hair.

"Hurry!" the woman screamed.

The juvenile sot knocked over a pile of wooden crates. "That should do it!" he said.

The woman backed away. "No. Absolutely not! I won't stand for it!"

"No, you'll sit for it." Spur grabbed the grandmother's waist. "Get in!"

"What do you think I am, a child?"

McCoy picked up the old woman and dumped her into the baby buggy.

Whistles from the approaching train pierced the air. Wind violently blew through the caboose.

"Now see here!" the woman yelled.

"This'll break your fall," Spur said. "Get off the tracks just after you hit. Move like you've never moved before, Granny!" he shouted. He pushed her to the back platform, hefted the buggy and tossed it over the railing.

"Holy shit!" the kid said as he stared at the approaching train.

"Go!"

They jumped together.

McCoy winced as the steel rail bit at his

shoulder. He rolled across the track and slid down the embankment that supported the tracks. The kid groaned nearby. Spur grabbed his belt and hauled him away as the elderly woman bellowed from the overturned buggy.

"Move your ass, kid!" Spur said as he dropped the boy. He ran to the overturned buggy, disengaged the woman and pulled her to safety.

The oncoming train's brakes roared. Two men leaped from the engine room seconds before the impact.

Spur flattened himself beside the grandmother.

The ironhorse slammed into the caboose. The ground shook and Spur's ears arched as tons of metal violently met. The caboose roared and jumped from its tracks. It split in two, listed and slid down the bank directly toward them.

"Shit!"

He dragged the shrieking grandmother from the caboose's path. Sand rained onto them from behind as the massive train car bounced and rolled. Metal crunched sickeningly as the caboose slammed to a halt in the sand.

It was over. Spur panted, lifted his head and had a look.

The caboose was half-buried. The bowed, squished rectangle would never again run the tracks.

The dining car lay on its side, crumbled and twisted in half. Surprisingly, the oncoming train hadn't suffered much damage. None of its cars had derailed during the collision.

Steam sprayed from the engine's windows. Flames flickered within it.

Passengers poured from the rear cars. Spur saw the kid from the caboose lying face-down. A black-uniformed man stormed up the sand. He glanced at the old woman and stared at Spur.

"My god, I'll have you arrested for this!" the gaunt man said. "If I had a weapon I'd take the law into my own hands! You damn near killed me, my crew and every ticketed passenger on my train!"

"Got one right here, boss," the fireman said.

Spur slapped his holster as the engineer took a familiar-looking revolver from his crewman's hand. The fall must have knocked McCoy's Colt .44 from his holster.

"You saying I planned this? To be caught in a runaway caboose with a kid and a grand-mother?"

"I don't care. You're responsible," he said, levelling the weapon.

"Put that thing away!"

The engineer turned. "Why should I, ma'am?"

"Because if you shoot him you'll have to shoot me too." She folded her arms and stood before Spur.

The beady-eyed man narrowed his brows. "No. No! You were his hostage! I saw him throw you off the train!"

"Hell, I was saving her life!" McCoy gently pushed her aside. "You aren't thinking straight. You're confused."

The engineer grunted.

"Why was your train so close to the 4:05? That's just plain dangerous!"

He stiffened. "That's none of your business. Don't keep changing the subject!"

"I'll tell you why it was so close!" The drunken caboose attendant rolled onto his back and stared up at the men. " 'Cause he was drinking. He's always drinking. That's why he messed up his schedule. Ask anyone."

The engineer dropped Spur's weapon. "Brad! What the hell are you doing here?"

Spur retrieved his revolver.

The boy stood, dusted off his clothing and turned to McCoy. "You see, my father never could stop drinking—even on the job. He taught me everything he knew about railroadin'. How many bottles to take with you, where to restock along the way. Ain't that right, old man?"

"Shut your mouth, son!" He clenched his hands into fists. "I haven't had a drink in five years!"

"Yeah? Then how come your train—the 3:30—is two hours early? You almost ran us down."

The engineer blubbered.

Spur shook his head. "You okay, kid?"

"Yeah. I'm fine."

"How about you, ma'am?"

The elderly woman crossed her arms. "Perfectly fit, thank you."

"Good. I'll need some help with the passengers. Some of them could have been hurt during the crash." Spur turned to the engineer. "And if I hear another word out of you I'll have you locked up!"

   "On what charge?"

   McCoy scowled. "Being alive!"

CHAPTER TWO

Spur rose at dawn and stretched. His hands banged against a solid wall. Yawning, he opened his eyes, rubbed them and got his bearings.

He was in a small, ornate room. Very small.

Sweet breath brushing across his chest hairs reminded him. The young woman who'd been on her way to meet her fiancé. The blue-eyed angel who'd taken one look at Spur and had invited him to share her compartment for his overnight stay.

Since the train had been in good shape, the passengers had spent the night in them. The bullish engineer had sworn to his frustrated customers that another train would be along first thing in the morning, and that he could arrange to have it take them back to its last stop.

McCoy kissed Annemarie's cheek and stood, popping the muscles in his back and shoulders, fully waking. In the distance he heard a faint whistle.

The morning train.

"Time to get up!" Spur yelled.

The young woman violently jerked into a sitting position. Red hair fell over her eyes. She stared at him through her scarlet veil.

"What's happening?"

Spur laughed and grabbed his clothes. "Our rescue approaches, little lady. I'd suggest you get dressed, as much as I hate to say it."

Annemarie nodded and flopped onto the mattress.

The woman was snoring by the time he was into his clothes. He tipped his Stetson at her and walked into the passageway.

McCoy went outside. He was surprised to see dozens of men, women and children standing in silence, watching the great sphere rise in the east. A preacher mumbled a prayer.

"There you are, McCoy!"

Spur groaned at the familiar voice. Engineer Taggert stomped up to him, wiping his hands together.

"Been saying your prayers?" he asked with a leer.

McCoy ignored the lewd comment. "So the train is coming after all," he said, turning to stare at the plume of smoke that approached them from the horizon. "That's the only thing you were right about yesterday."

"Okay, okay," the engineer said. He scratched the white and black stubble that had sprouted on his cheeks and chin and spat on the ground. "So I was out of my head."

"And drunk."

"I wasn't thinking straight. You can't blame a man for that."

"Right."

Taggert winced. "I just came up here to say I was—hell, forget it."

"Done!"

Something near Taggert's feet caught Spur's eye. He looked down. A small scorpion daintily walked up the engineer's boot, its tail raised.

"Ah, Taggert," he said.

"What?"

Spur caught his arm. "Shake your left leg."

The engineer guffawed. "Hell. You askin' me to dance? I think you're the one who's been drinking—mistaking me for a saloon gal."

"Shake it! There's a scorpion on your boot! It's walking up into your pants!"

The man blanched, though and smiled. "Hell, you're tryin' to hoodwink me. You're lower than a snake."

The deadly insect crawled higher and disappeared.

Spur didn't hesitate. He grabbed Taggert's broad shoulders and wrenched him back and forth. The surprised engineer pawed at him.

"What the hell you doing?"

"Trying to save your worthless life!"

The scorpion fell harmlessly onto the sand. Taggert jumped back and stared at it.

"I'll be a son-of-a-bitch!" he said. "You weren't lying! Thanks, McCoy."

"Maybe I shouldn't have told you." He

grinned and walked off to hurry Annemarie.

Ten minutes later, a train braked to a halt fifteen-feet from the assembled passengers. Heated words between the two engineers finally paid off.

"All aboard!" a weary conductor yelled.

Spur joined the human stream piling onto the train, tugging on Annemarie's sleeve. The new passengers sat wherever they found space—on the floor, on tables, in seats. A few minutes later the big iron horse reversed its engines and chugged back to its last stop— Deadridge, Arizona Territory.

The ride was short. Standing, Spur bent to look out a window. A crumbled mission lay in the distance. They were nearing the place. He ignored the crying babies, the fistfight that broke out over a seat and the heat of the car. McCoy thought about Annemarie and their night together.

Less than an hour later the train returned to the dingy little town of Deadridge. After disembarking, Spur registered at the only hostelry in town. He left Annemarie at the front desk of the Deluxe Hotel, dropped off his carpetbag in his room and looked for a telegraph office.

To his surprise he found one. McCoy sent a short, cryptic message to his superior, General Halleck, informing him of his whereabouts and why he hadn't begun working on his next assignment.

McCoy knew that the Secret Service would understand. He'd be stuck in the dusty town for two days if the trains ran on time, and from what he'd heard that wasn't likely to be the case. At least Annemarie would be nearby.

The one-eyed telegraph operator winked at him as he took Spur's money. "You stop by later to see if there's a response, sonny," he said.

Spur nodded and trudged into the sizzling sunlight. Somewhere in the vast expanses of Arizona Territory or California was a crafty thief who'd robbed fifteen banks in two months. He'd have to wait to start tracking him down.

McCoy sighed as he studied the dusty town. Maybe his blue-eyed angel wanted breakfast.

Burt Buxton tried on the gloves. They were of the finest leather, so supple he could pick up a pin. The black beauties were perfect.

"Burt, Burt," he said to himself. "You're smarter than any of them."

Buxton sat on the bed, lit a cheroot, puffed and threw the burning smoke into a spittoon. His boots treaded the floorboards from the door to the window, from the bed to the dresser, back and forth, up and down in a mindless pattern he'd long ago created.

Burt Buxton stopped. "Don't get your balls in an uproar," he said, catching his reflection in a badly silvered mirror. "It'll do no good."

The man who stared back at him looked older than the bookeeper who'd left Savannah six months ago. Was it really him, he wondered? That wild-haired, ragged-bearded loser wearing dirty clothes and a bullet-scarred hat?

The fine new gloves looked out of place. Buxton laughed and took them off. He threw them beside the gold pocketwatch and the other vestiges of civilization he'd recently obtained.

Think about work, he told himself.

Burt Buxton opened his suitcase, removed its contents and peeled off the cloth-covered cardboard bottom. He retrieved the map, spread it on the bed and sat, studying it.

The lines, squares, stars and diamonds wouldn't make sense to anyone else. They might even pass it off as doodles, never realizing that it was a diagram of the banks he'd robbed and the places where he'd hidden the money.

Just one more job, he told himself, tapping the blank area of the map where he hoped he'd draw another star. The Deadridge Bank. It should be simple.

It was a crude frontier town. It had no marshall, no local law enforcement. As usual, Buxton had checked into the town's history to see if it was a good place for him to go, and to satisfy his curiosity of why anyone would live in the middle of nowhere.

In centuries past, the springs that bubbled up in the area had been used by the local Indians. When the Spaniards pushed through the area they established a mission. By 1765 they'd converted the bulk of the Indians and had driven away those who wouldn't succumb to the true faith.

The Indians carved a white man's town of sorts from the relentless desert, laying out streets and building houses. Folks from back east started streaming through the area on their way to the far west. Suit-wearing Indians opened businesses to cater to the travelers. Soon the town of Deadridge—named for a sheer cliff that hung over the area—was firmly established.

The railroad had brought new wealth to the town. Rich men moved in and searched the rugged mountains for gold, silver and the legendary hordes of buried treasure that never seemed to be found.

And so Deadridge was a reality. Buxton had seen the mission from the train on his way in— the crumbling white walls had shown starkly against the brown desert varnish. The monks had left as soon as the saloons—and the women—had started to arrive and stay.

Burt Buxton tugged off his ragged clothes. He slipped into his best suit, straightened his bolo tie, slathered his hair with bearfat lotion and even splashed some bay rum on his neck.

He had all day, Buxton thought as he left his hotel room and locked the door. He never made his bank withdrawals until midnight.

"What is it? Go away!" The girl's voice was shrill.

"Annemarie, it's me, Spur McCoy!"

"I—I don't care. I can't see you right now!"

He stared at the closed door. That was strange. Last night she couldn't get enough of him. Maybe it was one of the womanly things. Was the moon full?

"Come on, Annemarie! Thought you might like some breakfast!"

"No!" she shrieked.

Spur frowned. "I'll come back later."

The door swung open. Annemarie stood wrapped in a woolen blanket. Her cheeks were pink and her forehead shone. "I really, I mean, heck, Spur. I'm busy." She nodded behind her and tightened the throw around her body.

A man sat up in bed. It took Spur a second to recognize him. "I—ah—didn't realize you two knew each other," McCoy said. "Sorry to disturb you, Taggert."

The crusty train engineer folded his arms. "You should be! Damn, just when it was getting good. Come on back here, little darling!"

The girl bit her lower lip. "I—I can't help it, Spur. I really can't! Maybe it's some sickness or something, but I've never been able to resist a man." She swallowed. "Almost any man!"

"Okay." Spur kissed her forehead. "I'll leave you to your prayers, Taggert," he yelled into the young woman's room. McCoy turned on his heel and left.

Deadridge. He had a feeling there was something to that name.

"Hey, McCoy!"

Spur automatically ignored the verbal invitation. Few people knew his real name, and most of them were behind bars or had been rotting below ground for some time. One of the first things he'd learned as an agent-in-training for the Secret Service was to choose when and where to respond to just such a situation.

He had to be on the alert at all times.

McCoy cautiously searched both sides of the street ahead, even though the voice had come from behind him. He ambled aimlessly through the horse-droppings that littered Deadridge's broad avenue.

A wagon slowly rattled on, driven by an immense man who dabbed his eyes. A plain pine coffin bounced behind him.

"You deaf or something, McCoy?"

That voice. Did he recognize it? Spur went through the long list of counterfeiters, shootists, confidence men, thieves, lady murderers, assassins, crooked politicians, fake preachers, medicine men and bull-headed ranchers that he'd dealt with in his years with the Secret Service. He couldn't quite remember hearing that voice before.

It was male, but high and thin. No trace of Southern accent. He was certain that if he'd ever heard that annoying squeak before he'd recognize it now.

"I'm getting tired of waiting!" the unseen man shouted.

McCoy slowed his steps and stopped in the center of the street. He casually tilted down the brim of his hat and walked to the nearest patch of shade, pulling a cigar from the pocket of his red and black plaid shirt.

Spur leaned against a pillar, enjoying the comparative coolness afforded by the roof that

stretched over the general store's porch. He
pretended to fumble in his pockets for a match
and turned.

Two Indian youths walked in, gripping a keg
of nails between them. A saloon girl, stumbling
as if shocked to see daylight, tripped over her
shadow and ran to the only dress shop in town.
An elderly man tried to grip his wife's
hand as they rocked away the morning on
the Deluxe Hotel's boardwalk. She pulled
away, embarrassed at the public show of
affection.

The only other person in sight—within
hearing range—was a gaunt, well-dressed man
who swung a lariat around his torso with
practiced ease.

Spur's eyebrows rose. The loop of rope
dropped over the man's torso and danced
around him.

The roper lifted his head. His face was
white.

Memories flooded through McCoy. It had
been one of his first assignments. St. Louis, he
remembered. He'd been looking for a bold thief
who'd pulled dozens of spectacular daylight
bank robberies.

He'd searched for the man who'd calmly
strangled every witness to his crimes before
leaving the scene, never even sparing the
women or children. He'd found him. Spur's
testimony had sent him to the gallows.

"You recognize me!" the thief said as he
stilled the rope and coiled it. "Fancy Freddie
Hardwick, back from the dead and twice as
slick!"

Spur drew. Before he could get a bead on the man a rope slid over his head from behind and tightened, biting into the tanned flesh of his neck.

CHAPTER THREE

The scratchy rope closed around Spur's throat. He twisted to face his unseen attacker but a solid blow to his kidney crumpled him to the ground.

A boot came down on his right hand. McCoy winced. The pain made him release the butt of his Colt .44. The same boot kicked it away.

He still hadn't seen the man who'd attacked him. Fred Hardwick advanced on him, throwing his coiled rope from hand to hand, broadly smiling.

Spur rubbed his bruised hand. The pressure around his windpipe loosened. He breathed deeply.

The man hadn't changed. Hardwick's face was still as pale as moonlight. White, curly hair hung to his shoulders. The killer stood over Spur and stared down at him, flashing his unworldly pink eyes.

The albino was alive.

"What the fuck do you want?" Spur yelled. "Aren't you supposed to be in hell by now? Roasting in some cauldron of boiling oil?"

Hardwick smiled. "Let's just say I have friends in higher places. Shit, McCoy. You think some cheap-ass prison can hold me, or that anyone could hang me? No. I've been hiding out for the last few years."

"You? Hiding out?" Spur snorted. The rope had gone slack. He stood. "Hardwick, you couldn't hide if you had to. You're so god-damned ugly that word spreads fast when you hit town. Men hide their daughters and stable their horses so they won't go berserk at the sight of you."

Hardwick tightened his white lips. "I see you haven't lost your genteel manners."

"Call off your man!" Spur said.

"You're in no position to give me orders. But I wasn't planning on snuffing out your miserable little life right here. No. I have bigger plans for you."

"Not if I have anything to say about it!" Spur grabed the noose, opened it and threw off the rope. He spun, slammed his fist into a surprised Indian's jaw and powered the man into the dust. In the same motion McCoy dove. He rolled on his shoulder and came up with his Colt .44 in both hands, its business end trained on Hardwick's chest.

"My, my. You certainly are something to watch!" the thief said.

"Don't move. If you even fart I'll blast you full of lead!" Spur's arms were steady. His finger teased the trigger of his revolver.

"Of course you will. But how would you explain that to your employers?" Hardwick raised his ivory right brow. "How can you kill me? I'm legally dead."

"You're standing right there!"

"Yes. They did hang Fancy Freddie Hardwick the day you left St. Louis. It was a drunken bastard my men found on the street. They bribed a sympathetic prison guard and I walked out before dawn. Strange as it might seem, the man looked quite a lot like me." The albino smiled.

"That must have broken his mother's heart," McCoy said.

Hardwick narrowed his eyes. "Kill me and Erick'll put a hole through your chest."

Spur glanced behind him. The Indian sat there, holding the handle of a Bowie knife between his thumb and forefinger. His grin displayed rotten teeth.

"Back off, McCoy!" Hardwick said. "This isn't the time. You'll know when it is!"

A young man on horseback rode up with an extra mount. Hardwick stepped into the saddle, kicked his mare's flanks and hastily rode away, leaving behind a grinning, knife-bearing Indian and an angry Spur McCoy.

"What the hell you lookin' at?" he asked Hardwick's hire.

The Indain sheathed his Bowie and walked away.

Pretty sure of himself, Spur thought as he stared at the departing outlaw. Fred Hardwick was still alive. The ruthless bank thief who'd terrorized dozens of small towns was still breathing.

Spur scraped brown goo from his boot sole and shook his head. Was there a connection between the latest string of bank robberies and Hardwick's sudden appearance? He'd have to find out before he moved on.

It didn't seem likely. The cryptic reports that General Halleck had sent to him from Washington stated that most of the robberies which he was supposed to investigate had taken place at night. All of the hold-ups had ended peacefully. There had been no mass killings.

It wasn't Hardwick's style, but maybe he'd changed his ways. Might as well find out how long Hardwick had been in town. If he'd been in Deadridge during the last bank robbery—in a hell-hole called Rio Verde—Spur could clear him. But if not . . . .

He started in the most likely place—the closest saloon. Two bits got him a glass of full-strength whiskey. Spur found a chair and sat.

McCoy grunted to the man who sat across from him. He looked out of place. He wore new city clothes and had the manner of a back-East gentleman, but his face was unshaven.

"Heard about some freak who came into town last few days," Spur said.

The man looked away and sighed.

"They say he's as white as snow, with red eyes and smile so slick it'd seduce a minister's daughter." Spur leaned toward the man. "Heard anything about him?"

"No." Ragged, uncut fingernails drummed on the table's surface. He wouldn't meet Spur's eyes. "Just got into town this morning."

"So did I." Spur guffawed and put on an act.

"Heard this fella's so goddamned ugly dogs won't even bite him, but the women say there's something about his eyes."

The drinker stared at him with smouldering eyes. "I'm sorry; I've heard nothing about it, sir!"

The violence of the man's response and his obvious disinterest in the subject convinced Spur that he was telling the truth. McCoy tipped his hat and left the table, searching for another likely source of information.

After the obnoxious man had left, Burt Buxton sighed and drained his glass. The last thing he wanted to do just hours before his next job was to listen to some wide-eyed idiot's tale of a human monster.

He picked up his glass, rose, sat it on the bar and walked out. There really was nothing to do here in Deadridge, he thought, eyeing its citizens with curiosity as they walked to and from various meaningless tasks.

Buxton turned and stared across the street at the Deluxe Hotel. An attractive woman dressed in shocking pink disappeared through its double doors, but Buxton's mind retained the image of her jiggling bottom long enough to truly enjoy it.

Who knows, he thought. Maybe he'd meet her.

Kitty Carson collapsed on the soft bed in her hotel room. She tugged at her pink dress, trying to reduce the discomfort of the impossibly tight garment. You've filled out, she said, throwing off her bonnet and letting it sail across the room. Time you got some new things.

Kitty let the mattress embrace her torso. She stared at the wallpaper that ran along the ceiling, noticing every small error that had been made during its placement.

The edges of the warmly brown wallpaper simply didn't line up. Bare plaster clearly showed through the irritating gaps. Work like that would never be tolerated back home.

But she wasn't at home. Stuck in a distressing hotel room in a backward town in Arizona Territory, Kitty shook her head as the memory of her latest terror overtook her.

The whistle had blown loudly. The train had braked in a drawn-out nightmare. Something was wrong, she'd thought.

The impact of the train's collision had sent her spiralling to the floor. The sound of shearing metal and the choruses of screams had been so terrifying that she'd covered her ears and waited to die.

It had finally ended. The car hadn't overturned as she'd feared and she was unharmed. Kitty had pulled herself up and calmly retrieved her purse and bonnet, which had become dislodged during the unfortunate meeting of her face and the floor. She'd pinned it into place and joined the stream of frightened passengers who hurried toward the exits.

Kitty Carson had hated the place on sight. It was even hotter than the last one-horse town she'd been in. The desert was so barren that even the cacti shriveled beneath the sun. Jagged, angry peaks surrounded the area. Far overhead, long-necked vultures rode the waves of intense heat that rose from the desert floor.

So this was Arizona! She hadn't imagined anywhere could be so inhospitable.

After a sleepless night in a chilly car, she'd crammed into the train that had unwittingly come to her rescue and suffered through the short trip back to Deadridge, a town which she'd thoughtfully avoided noticing on their way through it by falling asleep.

Now, twenty-four hours after the crash, Kitty Carson frowned at the ceiling and unconsciously pinched her cheekbones, something she'd done since her mother had forbidden her to wear rouge at the tender age of eight.

The twenty-two year old woman sighed and fanned her face with the dusty bonnet. She knew there wasn't a fresh flower within a hundred miles of this dump. That alone was enough to make her grab the fastest horse she could find and ride out of town. Or, she would if she could ride one of those ungainly beasts.

Kitty sighed at the thought and frowned. She rubbed her forehead and held back the scream that threatened to rip from her throat.

Calm down, she told herself, taking deep breaths. You'll have to change your plans. It wasn't like anyone was waiting to meet you in Yuma, she thought. No person, at least.

She practiced her smile, lifting her cheekbones, pressing together her firm lips. Kitty Carson sat up, planted her pearl-buttoned boots on the floor and walked to the window.

So maybe this wasn't San Francisco, she thought. At least you're not stuck all alone in the desert with bandits on your trail, with an empty canteen and very little food. With—with snakes wrapping around your neck and the heat burning your skin to blisters.

The comparison lifted her spirits. The woman sat and brushed her chestnut-colored hair, working the boar bristles through her shining mane. Her hair color was the only thing she'd gotten from her mother that meant anything to her.

The young woman sighed. Should I just waste this day waiting for the next train, she wondered? She thought of the options. She could always go to work.

Most small-town saloons were happy to get a new girl, even just for one night. It was a possibility.

She crossed her legs and worked a snag in her hair with the brush.

Of course, Kitty thought, she could go back to her other profession. The danger, the fear, and the final, generous reward was tempting.

The thought lit her emerald eyes.

Spur kicked at the dirt and leaned against a shaded post. The day had been a complete waste of time. He closed his eyes and filled his lungs as a carriage rattled by.

He had learned absolutely nothing during his investigation into Fred Hardwick. He'd talked to dozens of men and women with no results. He'd gone to every store in town. None of the owners or employees recalled seeing a male albino, and none said they'd sold anything to one in the last few weeks. A few of them didn't even know what an albino was.

Frustrated, he'd checked the rest of the saloons. No clues. His inquiries were met with blank stares. An albino in town? the man had said. Never seen one of them around here.

The saloon girls hadn't been any help either. The sad-eyed women blankly shook their heads at his question and returned to their endless search for new customers.

He'd actually found two people who'd been on the street earlier that day and had witnessed Fred Hardwick suddenly challenging McCoy. Both of them, however, couldn't recall seeing his face. One man had explained, "We keep to ourselves here. Don't get involved with trouble."

McCoy had questioned them as roughly as he could but, once again, had gained no information. The men were either lying or had their own reasons for not telling the truth.

He'd run into dead-ends all day. About noon he'd gone to send a new wire to his boss to explain that Fred Hardwick was still alive, was in Deadridge, and that he suspected the man might be responsible for some or all the bank robberies he was supposed to be investigating.

But the one-eyed telegraph operator had told him that the lines were down a few miles east from town. Nothing could go out or come in for at least a few days.

Hot, tired and frustrated, Spur tried to track down the local unofficial lawman—an ornery cuss by the name of Buck Frazier. He soon learned that Buck had left Deadridge last week, following the trail of a man who'd apparently slept with his wife and his teen-aged daughter.

McCoy shrugged as he stared at the deep blue sky. He sure as hell hadn't imagined he'd ever seen the white-haired madman. But he was alive, and he was in Deadridge.

Spur recalled the man's brilliant white face, the piercing pink eyes and his high-pitched voice. The memory made him scowl. He sent a wad of saliva to the sand. It sputtered and evaporated from the heat.

Hardwick might have escaped hanging once, he thought, but this time nothing would stop him from bringing the outlaw to justice.

All he had to do was find him.

Spur pounded his fist into his left hand. Someone who looked like Fred Hardwick simply couldn't hide in a town the size of Deadridge.

But then, the man had always done the impossible.

CHAPTER FOUR

The street outside his hotel window was sleepy. Burt Buxton slipped into his calf-length black coat, tucked a black hat on his head and went off to work.

He'd watched the bank close an hour before sunset. The owner, a stocky, bald, sway-backed man, paced around the exterior of the building for several minutes, endlessly puffing on a cigar. He peered into windows. He rattled the knobs on both the front and back doors four times. Finally, he'd walked away, leaving the bank alone as the sun wrapped it in deepening shadows.

Now, just after ten p.m., Burt Buxton kicked at a tumbleweed that dustily rolled toward him in the street. He patted the small lump under his coat, checking to make sure that he had his revolver.

Of course it was there.

This was his seventh robbery in two months, but Buxton felt his chest tighten as he turned a corner and saw the Deadridge Bank before him. A young family walked by, the mother and father trying to corral their four children.

"You're gonna get a whippin' when we get home!" the man said.

"Am not! I'll whup your ass!"

"Jason!" the harassed mother shrieked.

The four boys shot down the street. Their parents followed them.

Buxton casually changed directions, headed past the gaudiest of the drinking and gambling establishments and entered a side street.

There were still too many people out there, he thought. His boot hit something solid in the inky blackness of the alley. It groaned.

A drunk. Some poor man must have thrown back too much whiskey. Buxton stepped over the sot, turned and went into the saloon.

Good idea.

Kitty Carson flipped a hand through her hair and tapped her boot on the floor. It was so early, she thought. And she had nothing to do.

The young woman looked at the trunk she'd brought with her. A length of ebony chiffon fell over its side and spread onto the bare wooden floor. She licked her lips. It *was* tempting, Kitty thought. Fun and excitement and money too. After all, she was here. Shouldn't she enjoy herself?

Of course. Just because some stupid runaway train had unavoidably changed her plans was no reason to sit all night in her hotel room. It was time she had some, ah, recreation. Why, how long had it been since the last time? A week? Maybe two weeks?

She glanced at her reflection in the mirror and shook her head. No, pink silk definitely wasn't right. It was much too ladylike for what she had planned.

There was the emerald green, a gown that fit her so tightly she could barely breathe. Kitty shivered at the thought of trying to get into a corset and settled on the black chiffon.

She hummed a civil war song as she busily unbuttoned. The pink silk slid to the floor. The woman's cheekbones rose and her lips creased as the chilly night air blew across her chemise and ruffled her petticoats.

She dragged the black dress over her head and pulled it into place. After a few moments of primping she turned to the mirror and sighed.

That wasn't going to work either.

Kitty looked into her trunk. She had one outfit left.

Might as well use that one again, she thought, as she took off the black chiffon.

Just after sunset, McCoy had watched the orange and red show in the western sky. The air cooled considerably, but heat still radiated from the buildings and sand around him.

Spur launched himself from the rocking chair that sat on the porch before the Deluxe Hotel. His boots dug into the sand that countless years of burning sunlight had deepened to a dull bronze hue. Didn't it ever rain here?

Fred Hardwick was damned exasperating, McCoy thought. The white-haired, white-skinned outlaw was living up to his reputation, even after his death.

The man was resourceful. Spur remembered how he'd chased Hardwick and his men for nearly a month before finally trapping them in the act of blowing a safe at the Riverdale Bank. McCoy, the sheriff and a deputy had shot at the robbers for nearly an hour before Hardwick had run out of ammunition. They'd already managed to put his four back-up men out of commission, so McCoy had simply walked in and knocked out Fred Hardwick with a fist to his glass jaw. The outlaw had then spent a cozy night in jail.

Three days later they were back in St. Louis. Hardwick had been convicted of five bank robberies and the murders of twelve innocent men, women and children. The bearded judge sentenced him to hang.

Spur's face burned as he remembered his last run-in with the notorious thief. It wasn't his job to try and convict criminals, just to deliver them. But he couldn't help wondering: if he'd stayed in St. Louis until after the hanging, would Fred Hardwick have escaped his punishment?

A lantern hanging from the porch of the Bourke Drinking Establishment swung in the breeze. The plaintive creak of its metal ring scraping through the top of the burning kerosene lantern irritated Spur so much that he turned and headed for the bank.

The building was dark gray, squat and looked secure. An owl violently fluttered from

the sky and perched on the finial that topped
the center of the bank's false front. There
wouldn't be any moonlight for an hour or two,
McCoy thought. It was the perfect time for a
robbery.

He looked across the street. Chester
Andrews had apparently received a new
shipment of something, judging from the pile
of empty barrels that lay scattered before
Andrews' Dry Goods Store. Spur crossed the
street and squatted behind them. He had a
clear view of the front of the bank.

With Fancy Freddie Hardwick in town,
maybe he should keep an eye on the place.

The sole lantern cast meager light in the huge
barn two miles out of Deadridge.

"Shut up!" Hardwick said.

Elijah Martin threw down his hat. "But boss!
It's just sitting there waiting for us! Who the
fuck cares if McCoy's in town? He can't find
you. No one can! We're farting away the whole
night!" the curly-haired youth said.

Fred Hardwick smiled and slapped his
second's shoulder. "You talking back to me,
boy?"

Elijah stepped away and lowered his head.
"No. I mean, well, shit, Hardwick!"

Fred stabbed the air with his forefinger.
"Never use that name! I've told you time and
again, from town to town! Jesus, Elijah, you're
making me wonder if hiring you on was such
a good idea."

The youth rubbed his hands, still studying
the straw-littered barn floor. "It was. Honest!"

He lifted his head to meet Hardwick's gaze.

Elijah cringed as the pink eyes fixed on his. The man wasn't human, he thought. But he paid well.

"Forget I ever said it, Mr. Hard—"

Fred raised his brows.

"Mr. Holton." Elijah forced a smile. "I just wanna go out with you again. To blow another safe. To rob another bank!"

Hardwick spat. "You're too eager, Martin. That'll get you dead faster than you can imagine. This isn't one of those games you used to play as a kid. These aren't popguns," he said, tapping his silver-handled revolver.

"I know. And I'm sorry."

"Good boy!" Fred Hardwick stepped closer to the pot-bellied stove. He opened the firebox. Red flames burst from it, forcing the outlaw backward. Hardwick stuffed a thick length of precious wood into the inferno, briefly warmed his hands near it and cut off the flaming sight by slamming shut the small door.

"Fetch some water," Hardwick said. "Take the pail there and work the pump out back."

Freed from the man's power, Elijah shook his head and scratched his ear. "Sure, but why? You thirsty or something, Mr. Holton?"

"No. You're going to take a bath."

The boy stepped back, tripped over a bale of hay and landed on his butt. His arms and legs slapped against the earthen floor. "What?"

Fred Hardwick laughed. "You know what I've been talking about for the last few weeks?"

Elijah nodded. His cheeks drained of color.

"Tonight's the night. Elijah H. Martin, you're going to have a woman before dawn! Now rustle up some water. The way you stink, no saloon girl would get within twenty feet of you! No matter how much I paid her."

"But Mr. Holton!" the youth said as he found his feet. "Tonight? You mean—"

Hardwick threw back his head and guffawed. "Can't you understand plain English!"

Elijah nodded. "Yes. I think!" He bent to clamp shaking fingers around the pail handle. A woman. A woman!

"Move your ass, boy!" Hardwick yelled. "Or you won't be moving her ass tonight!"

Spur stretched his legs. He'd gotten to know the backside of every barrel that had stood before him. No one had approached the bank. A few men had passed by it, but none had even turned a head toward the building.

Things were quiet.

Maybe Hardwick wouldn't make his move tonight. Before his arrest and, uh, execution, he always did his work in broad daylight. He had seemed to especially enjoy killing the witnesses. His men sometimes helped out, but Hardwick usually did it himself. The bastard probably assured them they wouldn't be hurt as he and his men stormed in. Then, after they'd cleaned out the safe, he'd killed them one by one, forcing the others to watch.

Fancy Freddie Hardwick, as he called himself, had never been caught because he took incredible risks. Few lawmen had figured that anyone would rob a bank in the afternoon while it was full of people. At that time the outlaw had had five men working for him. Two would be outside, keeping anyone from coming in and standing by ready with the horses. It had never taken more than a few minutes to rob any bank that he'd hit.

During the investigation that had lead to Hardwick's eventual arrest, Spur had learned something of the way the man worked. He'd move into a town about a week before with his "friends." His unusual coloring had always attracted much attention, but he'd been so free with money that the citizens had always accepted him as a new resident.

Before the actual robbery he'd ridden all over the surrounding area, finding the quickest routes out of town, the best places to hide out if necessary. He'd find trails across streams and through vegetation.

During the robberies he and his men usually dressed alike. Even their horses were similar in coloring and size. After the robbery, they'd split up to confuse anyone that may be following them, to meet again at some distant place. Hardwick always carried all the money.

Spur had finally caught one of his men and had persuaded him to tell everything he knew. It seemed the outlaw, one Tompkin, had fallen out with Hardwick the night before they'd pulled the job. He had planned to leave him right after he'd gotten his share. McCoy hadn't believed what had caused the split—Hardwick demanded to watch his men make love with women—the uglier the better.

Tompkin's agonized confession had finally led to the outlaw's arrest. He'd known where the next hold-up would be, and McCoy had waited there for Hardwick.

Spur rubbed his calves and resumed his

squatting position. A dark figure approached the bank. A metallic sound issued from the man.

Keys, he thought? Hardwick wouldn't have keys.

Or would he?

Spur rose as the figure opened the door and walked inside.

He just might.

CHAPTER FIVE

The bank door closed as the figure walked in. Spur ran across the street, slipped up to the darkened building and tried the knob. It turned.

He went inside. A sliver of light splashed onto the bank floor from the door. The shadowy figure went to what looked like a desk and turned to face him.

"Who's there?" it demanded in a husky voice.

Spur had already drawn. "Who the hell are you? I'll ask the questions!"

"Nothing doing! This is my bank, asshole!" Glinting metal swung up in the figure's hand.

"How do I know you're not breaking in?" Spur said, maintaining his aim.

"With the keys? You were obviously watching me." The figure approached him and stepped into the moonlight. A rifle stretched out of his hands, trained at Spur's chest. "You better talk fast, asshole!"

"I'd agreed that, under the circumstances, that would be best."

The figure snorted. "You sure as hell don't sound like a thief."

"I'm not." Spur trusted his instincts. This obviously wasn't Fancy Freddie Hardwick. And he hadn't had a rifle with him when he'd walked in; it must have been placed on the desk before closing.

He gently lowered the tip of his revolver. "I'm Spur McCoy, Secret Service. I'm investigating a string of bank robberies that have occurred throughout California and Arizona Territory. A known outlaw's in town, so I was watching the bank."

"Uh-huh."

Silence.

"I figured it might be robbed tonight."

"Maybe it would have been . . . if my deadly friend hadn't been here." He waved his rifle.

Spur grinned. He still couldn't see the figure's face. A kerosene lamp sat on a nearby marble counter. "Mind if I shed some light on the situation?" he asked.

The gunman grunted affirmatively. "If you try anything you won't get another chance."

Spur slowly reached into his pants pocket and extracted a lucifer. He struck it on his boot, held up the flaring, exploding stick and walked to the counter. A second later yellow light bloomed in the bank. Spur pushed the chimney into place, raised the wick and turned to face the gunman again.

He was a beefy, red-faced, bald man, so fat that any horse would protest having him on its back. The thin light caught fine sweat on his face, making it shine. The man waved his rifle to the right.

"Sit!" he bellowed.

Spur dropped into the chair.

"Okay. McCoy, was it?"

He nodded.

"McCoy, you talk a pretty good story. And I didn't catch you doing anything. But why should I let you go?" Steel-blue eyes peered at him.

He didn't look a thing like Freddie Hardwick. "So your bank won't be robbed later tonight. Or tomorrow night!"

Still fifteen-feet away, the man chewed his lower lip. "Secret Service, huh?"

"Right."

"I heard of them. Old Bud Myles down to Tucson had some trouble with phoney money a while back. Some guy from the Secret Service came to help him out."

Spur smiled at the distant memory. "What was the agent's name?"

The gunman screwed up his face, nibbled his lower lip and stared at the ceiling. He finally lowered his head. The soft light caught his astonished expression.

"McCoy. Spur McCoy! That was the name of the gent who helped him out!"

Spur smiled. "Can I get up now?" He stood before the man could respond. "What's your name?"

The banker placed his rifle on the desk. "The name's Ames. Curly Ames."

McCoy walked to him and took the bald man's hand. "Must be an old nickname. Ames, I wasn't here to break into your bank. I was here to see if you were breaking in."

"I figure. Shit, my brain's aching!" he said. "Don't know what to think!"

"What brought you back here this time of night? You've been closed for hours."

Ames slid his thumbs behind the waistband of his pants and tugged outward, trying to find room for his stomach. "Forgot to do some figures," he said, motioning to the desk.

"So you'll be working."

He nodded. Three chins bobbed up and down.

"You want me to keep an eye on the place—from the outside, I mean?"

Ames spread his arms. "Don't bother yourself, McCoy. Go get some sleep. I'll stay here myself until morning. It'll probably take me that long to get these numbers straight." He sat behind the desk and lit a second lamp. "Me and my friend here'll be just fine."

"You sure?"

Curly tapped his Spencer repeating rifle's barrel. "Yeah, I'm sure. Pleased to make your acquaintance, McCoy. I've heard a lot about you."

"Same here, Ames. Keep your eyes open, okay?"

The banker laughed as Spur trotted out.

Two hours later, the circle of light surrounding the desk narrowed. The lantern's wick had absorbed every drop of the kerosene. The spluttering flame cast shadows across Curly Ames' bald pate.

The lamp went out. Saliva drooled from his lips as Ames snored.

Burt Buxton stuffed his gloved hands into his pocket, left the saloon and strode behind it. The bank was just two buildings down. He patted his revolver's handle and smiled through the darkness.

It was well past midnight.

A horse, spooked, whinneyed far away. Burton sighed. He'd never run into trouble before. He'd never been challenged or stopped during any of his bank robberies. And this one wouldn't be different.

He rounded the rear of the barber shop. The bank stuck out twenty-feet closer to the unending desert. Whoever had built it had used adobe bricks. Solid. Tough.

But, against all reason, the builder had installed a back door. It was perfect for Buxton's purposes—out of direct sight from the street, facing nothing but open sand.

Buxton's heels mushed softly on the ground as he approached the rear of the bank. He glanced down the alley between it and the barber shop as he passed it. No lights shone in its windows. But why would anyone be there at this time of night?

His glove softly squeaked as he gripped the cold knob. Buxton winced at the sound and tried to turn his hand. It was locked.

Burt reached into his pocket and pushed a skeleton key into the hole directly below the brass orb. It went in. He jiggled it. Something gave. The knob spun in his hand.

He slipped the skeleton key into his coat pocket, swung open the door and walked inside.

He stepped silently through the storeroom, passing piles of ledgers, books and canvas bags. His throat tightened. He walked through the doorless opening into the bank itself.

The safe was just beside him. It was a small thing—a MacDonald and Stewart. No more than three-feet high. Fancy gold lettering and curlicues graced its front.

Buxton didn't glance around the elongated room. He squatted and went to work on the dial, one ear pressed to the safe's door, the other twirling the knob that would keep him living well for another month or two.

Kitty smiled and swaggered down the boardwalk. A man shuffled by on his way into a saloon. She poked an ivory toothpick between her front teeth and walked in.

No one even noticed her. She blended in so well that she was nearly invisible. The young woman tucked a bit of hair back under her hat and went on.

This was more like it, she thought, slapping at her ill-fitting clothes. Nothing was too tight. There were no stays or corset to strangle her lungs and grip her ribs.

True, dressed as she was, Kitty wasn't the image of femininity, but it suited her purpose. At least she was comfortable.

And she was wearing a gunbelt.

*   *   *

Spur slapped at a moth that had been flapping around his face for at least an hour. The white insect shot away from him through the air.

He could be snoring away in bed by now instead of watching the Deadridge Bank. He was sure that Curly could take care of things himself.

Yellow light still shone through the front window, though it had gotten fainter.

If he didn't get some sleep soon he wouldn't be in much condition to search for Fred Hardwick. Spur had already changed his plans; he wasn't leaving Deadridge until he'd faced the man again.

Unwilling to walk away from the post, McCoy stifled a yawn and stretched. Maybe just a little nap, he thought, as his chin sunk to his chest.

Kitty Carson had already decided not to use the front entrance. She skirted the building and was pleased to discover a back door. Her hand closed around the knob. It turned.

Alarmed, Kitty considered the situation. Should she go in? Maybe they'd just forgotten to lock it. Maybe it didn't have a lock. Or maybe this was such a small town that they actually didn't lock the doors at night.

Don't be stupid, she told herself. Her rough clothing seemed to give her confidence. Kitty straightened her back and slipped inside.

The dim light told her she was in some kind of anteroom. The brown-haired beauty carefully moved across the floor. A doorway yawned before her. She walked through it and nearly shrieked in surprise.

A man bent near the safe, busily working it. He looked up.

Kitty turned to run.

"What are you doing here?" the man said in a whisper. He stood and instantly drew. "This is my bank! Get yer ass outa here!"

"I—I—" Kitty blushed. She clumsily reached for her holster.

"I said, git!" the thief whispered. "Or you'll never walk out of here alive!"

"But!"

The thief cocked his head. "This your first time?"

Kitty's Stetson went up and down, then side to side. She trembled.

"Let me get a look at you, boy."

The young woman stepped back. "No. I'll— I'll be leaving now."

"Suit yourself, boy! You'd better leave this kind of work to grown men!"

Kitty nodded. She quietly stepped into the back room, her chest pounding. What bad luck, she thought. To break into a bank that was being broken into!

"Hold it a second!" the man behind her said. "Get back here!"

She turned. Her hips bumped a table. Its stiff leg screeched across the floor.

"Quiet!"

"That you, Spur?"

The sleep-slurred words emanating from the darkness of the bank made them both freeze.

"Holy shit!" the man said. He grabbed Kitty's arm. "Are you Spur?"

She shook her head.

"Then who the fuck's that?"

"Answer me, Spur!"

They hesitated.

A rifle exploded and dislodged a chunk of adobe from the wall behind them.

The man grabbed Kitty's hand. They shot through the doorway and ran from the bank.

Her unused muscles resisted the thief's constant strain but she went with the nameless man, pouring her fear into the effort to find safety.

"Move it! I got a horse nearby!"

"Okay—okay!" Kitty said in a breathless, high voice.

"Jeez, kid! You sound like you're twelve years old!"

Kitty didn't argue. They sped through the soft, sucking sand. She willingly followed him, running like she hadn't run since she was a little girl.

They rounded the barber shop and headed onto the street. The thief dropped her hand.

"Keep up with me!" he yelled.

A horse stood at a trough up ahead. It sniffed the air at their approach and pranced. The man had her reins untied and was in the saddle by the time Kitty arrived. A strong hand gripped hers. The ground spun away from her boots. She sat on the hard leather and grabbed his waist.

A rifle sounded behind them.

The horse took off. Deadridge blurred on either side. Kitty held on as the thief and his frisky mount sped her from the bank and into the unknown.

CHAPTER SIX

"Damn!"

The discharge of a rifle blasted Spur into total consciousness. He stood, drew, leaped from behind the barrels and ran across the street to the bank.

"Ames!" he shouted. The door was locked. The rifle sounded again from behind the building.

Spur ran down the alley. No one passed its exit as he approached. McCoy cleared the alley. A man rushed from the bank's back door—the *back door?*

"Hold it!" Curly Ames shouted at him, levelling his weapon.

"Christ, Ames! It's me, McCoy! What's happening?"

"There was two of them. In my goddamned bank!" The man dashed through the sand.

Hardwick, Spur thought, as he grabbed his hat and followed. "Did they get the safe open?"

"No. Wait a minute. Fuck! I forgot to lock the door!" A silver object arced over Ames' shoulder and jangled to the ground. "You get it for me, McCoy!"

The banker was soon out of sight around the barber shop's rear wall.

Spur ran past the keys, looked up, ran back to them and clasped the cold metal ring in his hand. Cursing, McCoy locked the back door of the bank and stormed onto the street.

Ames stood alone in its center, reloading, stomping the ground.

"Damn it!" he yelled.

"Where are they?"

Curly spun to face him. "How in hell would I know?"

"You got a horse?"

The man nodded, then shook his head. "Damnit! She threw a shoe this afternoon. Sam, the farrier's, out sick himself, so I was waiting until tomorrow."

Spur thought. He hadn't rented a horse, but then, he hadn't had any reason to. "Any place we could get a horse?"

Ames snorted. "This late? No. There aren't too many extra ones around. Had a horse-thief sweep through here a month ago. Since then men've been sleeping beside them." He gestured around him. "You see any of those soulless beasts tied up on the street?"

He didn't. The hitching posts were empty. Even at midnight there were usually a few nags tied up here or there. But there wasn't a horse in sight.

Spur threw the keys to Curly Ames. "At least the bank's locked up. You got a good look at them?"

"Hell no!" Ames waddled up. "It was near pitch black. I must've nodded off. Then that damned lamp burned out. I heard voices and fired. Then ran!" He wiped his hatless brow. "I thought it was you at first, checking up on me. What the hell are you doing here anyway?"

"I was across the street in front of the dry goods store keeping an eye on the bank. Didn't know you had a back door. What idiot put up that building?"

Ames spat. "I did! The back door's come in handy more than once. Deliveries, pick-ups of large amounts of cash. Never thought it would nearly wipe me out."

"And the town's assets. Better get that thing boarded up or bricked over."

Curly Ames kicked the dirt. "Hell, McCoy, we can't just stand here!"

"If there's no horses to be gotten let's go back to your bank and look around. There might be something that'd help us out."

"Anything'd be better than this."

They returned to the back door. Ames let them in.

"There were two men. I know you didn't get a clear view of them, but did you notice anything?"

"No." Ames knelt beside the safe and tried the dial. He sighed. "Thank the good Lord it's still locked up tight." He peered at the circle of numbers and struck a match. "But he was good. The tumbler's resting on the first number."

"Curly!"

The man shot him a look. "What in tarnation is it?"

"Was there anything about them that made you—" Spur sniffed the air. "That made you—what in hell is that?"

"What?" Ames demanded as he stood.

"I'm smelling something. It's all over the fuckin' place! Just under the stench of gun-powder."

"The dust gets caught up my nose," Ames said, shaking his head. "Can't smell a dad-blamed thing. Kerosene, maybe? I did have the lamp lit."

"That isn't kerosene." Spur smelled again and snapped his fingers. "Perfume! Jesus, it's perfume!"

Ames drew back his chin. "You're plumb crazy, McCoy! What kinda bank robbers wear perfume?"

Spur shrugged. "You sure there were two men?"

"Yeah. At least, they were both wearing pants."

"And you didn't see anyone else?"

"No. But it was dark, and I was just waking up. Just what are you getting at, McCoy?"

He sniffed again. "I'm not sure. But if I were you, I'd hire on some guards to watch this place day and night. You know some trust-worthy men?"

Ames nodded. "Sure! There's Felix. He used to work for me before he up and—"

"Good. Get two of them. Arm them. Have them stand watch inside during the day, outside at night. Keep this place locked up, lights burning from sunset to sunrise."

"Sure, sure. But what the hell are you gonna be doing?" Ames asked.

"I smell a rat. And I'm gonna find him—or her."

"Her?" Curly snorted.

"Slow down!" Kitty said as the horse bucked beneath her. She tightened her grip around the man's midsection. "Where are we going?"

He turned to yell in her ear. "What do you care? Move your hands a little lower, honey! You'll grab my crotch!"

She released his torso and nearly fell from the mare. Kitty gently grasped his sturdy form. "What?"

"You can forget the act, missy. I knew you were a woman the second you pressed your chest against my back. And besides that, you've got enough perfume on to make twelve saloon girls smell pretty for a week."

Wind slammed into Kitty's blushing cheeks. She eased from him but couldn't find room on the saddle. "So?"

He reined in the horse and looked behind him. Deadridge was at least two miles away. The rising moon showed no signs of a pursuit.

Burt Buxton twisted around and faced her. "So what in hell were you doing in that bank?"

Kitty licked her lower lip. "Ah, well, I was making a deposit?"

"More like a withdrawal." Buxton laughed. "That feels good, your legs wrapped around my thighs." He pushed his buttocks against her crotch. "Real good!"

The emerald-eyed woman cringed. "You

animal! Get away from me!"

Kitty struggled against the intimate pressure. Her body tilted. Buxton laughed.

The woman yelped as she lost her balance and slid sideways from the saddle. The man stared down at her as she brushed off her pants and tried to stand in the ankle-deep hollow of sand.

"Who in Hades are you?" she demanded.

"Burt Buxton, at your service." He touched the brim of his hat. "And now, would you mind telling me who's pretty little ass I just saved?"

Kitty looked up at him and planted her hands on the sand. "Help me out of here and I just might do that."

Buxton stepped from the saddle, extended a hand and pulled her to her feet.

"Thank you. I'm Kit Carson."

Burt roared.

"I mean—Kitty Carson."

"Kitty Carson?"

"Yes." She dislodged the sand that had adhered to her leather vest. "That's my, ah, professional name."

"I see." Buxton took out two cheroots. "Would you like a smoke, sir?" he asked, staring at her masculine clothing.

Kitty shook her head.

"No? Then I'll have one, sir."

He pocketed the second and lit the thin cigar. When he was freely puffing Burton held the match to her face.

"I'll be you're a looker when you're not dressed up like a man, sir," he said.

Kitty stepped away from him. "Stop calling me that! I'm not a man! I'm a woman!"

He tossed the match. "Really? How do I know you're not just a well-padded gelding?"

Her cheeks burned. "A—a *what*?"

Buxton laughed. Kitty set her jaw, went to him, grabbed his hand and laid it lightly over her right breast. The man raised an eyebrow.

"Is that padding, Mr. Buxton?"

"Ah, er, I guess not. Definitely not." His fingers extended over the warm lump that lay beneath her plaid cotton shirt and leather vest.

She squeaked and threw back his hand. "What do you think you're doing?" Kitty demanded.

"Just checking out the competition, ma'am."

The moonlight slanting across the desert floor illuminated his face. He was amused.

"Competition?" She shook her head and crossed her arms. "I know what you were doing. What kind of a woman do you think I am?"

Buxton approached her. "How should I know? A woman who interrupts me while I'm trying to open a bank safe? Who's a man one minute, then changes her sex? A woman who forces me to paw her like an unlettered, debased savage?"

"Okay, so I'm kinda complicated. I don't know! Nothing's gone right since the train wreck and—"

Buxton cut her off. "Don't tell me you were responsible for that too!"

Kitty shook her head. "No. Were you on the train?"

"Hardly. Rode in here on horseback." He put his hands on his hips. "So now, Kitty Carson, what the hell am I going to do with you?"

She stared at the star-speckled sky. "Prove to me that you're a man, I guess. That way neither of us'll be confused."

"Very well." Burt Buxton took her hand in his glove and moved it toward his crotch. Kitty shivered as he pressed it against a warm lump.

"Need more proof?" he asked.

She put her free arm around his shoulder. "Sure. You can prove it to me all night long."

Fred Hardwick stood motionless in the corner of the foul-smelling room above the saloon. The girl was exceptionally ugly. Coarse brown hair fell around her monstrous nose, beady eyes, sloping forehead, jutting chin and cracked, broken teeth.

"Well go on, Elijah!" Hardwick said. "Rip off her dress."

The youth fidgeted as he stood in his long underwear.

"Hey! Nothing doing!" the whore yelled. "Unless you pay me for it too."

Her gruff voice furthered Hardwick's interest in her. "Okay." He handed her a ten-dollar gold coin.

The saloon girl bit it, flipped it onto the nightstand and spread her arms.

"Go ahead, junior," she said to the youth. "Do it!"

Elijah trembled. Hardwick leaned over him.

"Get that bitch naked or you'll never do another job for me!"

The boy nodded. He grabbed a fold of cloth. The whore laughed as her dress split in two and fell to the floor. Hardwick shrugged as she stood naked before them. She was curved in all the right places. The face was the best part of her, he thought.

"Now go to it, kid!" he said.

Hardwick shoved Elijah. The boy fell onto the saloon girl and both of them slammed onto the bed.

"Come on, honey," she said. "Nothing to be afraid of. Ain't I pretty enough for you?"

"Sure, you're pretty enough for him," Hardwick said. "You're the goddamndest prettiest woman I've ever seen!"

Elijah grunted and yanked at his single garment. His gyrations quickly freed his body of the long underwear. Hardwick stood closer as the youth stretched on top of the whore.

"Shove it in! Goddamn it, Elijah! Do it!"

The whore laughed.

Elijah did it.

CHAPTER SEVEN

It wasn't Fancy Freddie Hardwick who'd tried
to rob the bank that night, Spur thought as he
returned to the hotel room. He couldn't quite
convince himself that Hardwick would have a
woman along with him, and the stench of
perfume in the air proved that a woman had
indeed been involved in the attempted robbery,
unless there were some mighty strange thieves
running around this part of Arizona Territory.

Just because Hardwick didn't seem to be
responsible for any of the bank robberies that
the Secret Service was interested in, didn't
mean that he hadn't done others. McCoy
couldn't imagine that the outlaw had been
twiddling his thumbs for the past several years.
He must have been working. Perhaps he had
done *some* of the robberies.

The outlaw's sudden appearance in

Deadridge that morning had been so unexpected that Spur didn't know what to think. He shrugged and went up the stairs of the Deluxe Hotel.

A woman appeared in the doorway of the room beside his. Smoke billowed behind her. The curtains were aflame.

"Help?" she said in a tiny voice.

"What's wrong?" A flickering orange and red phantom rose from her rear. "You're on fire!"

"I—I—"

Spur shoved the thin woman to the floor. He rolled her back and forth, smothering the flames that had been licking her simple, homespun dress. When they'd gone out Spur stood, ripped the burning curtains from their rod and stomped on them. Thick soot and whisps of blackened material drifted up from beneath his boots. Spur extinguished every hot spot, sighed and turned to the woman.

"Are you alright, ma'am?"

The young woman lifted her head and blubbered. Tears spilled from her violet eyes. She tossed her long black hair.

"Did you get burned?"

"No," she said, "but the room's a mess!"

She was a pretty thing, Spur thought as he grinned and hauled her up. The girl rubbed her nose, looked at the destroyed curtains and burst into tears again.

"No need for that," he said.

McCoy gripped her shoulders. She melted and wrapped her delicate arms around his chest. The young woman pressed her face to his chest. She was short, he thought.

"Tell me what happened," he said gently, rubbing her hair.

"I knocked over the lamp and it caught the curtains on fire and—and—"

"It could have happened to anyone." He patted her back. The flesh beneath her flimsy white gown was tense.

"I know, but we don't have much money! I can't pay for that and—and—"

"Hush, child." Spur soothed her with his strong hand until she'd quieted.

He held her at arm's length. "Look at me," he said kindly.

The girl did. Huge lavender eyes took him in. Her reddened nose was turned up at the end, small and just the right size. High cheekbones and a small chin, framed with rich black hair, completed the picture.

"Why, you're not a little girl," Spur said, glancing below her head. "You're a woman!"

"I know." She wiped her eyes. "I'm Patti O'Brannigan. My father's out of town. He never trusts me alone out at the ranch, so he put me up here in the hotel for a week. And now he'll have to pay for all of this—this—" Her lower lip quivered.

"Pull yourself together, woman! Crying won't accomplish a thing."

She responded to the harshness of his voice. Patti nodded and held her chin high.

"That's much better." Spur grinned at her. "When's your father coming back?"

Patti sighed. "Tomorrow or the next day. He didn't know for sure. But we have two men looking after our ranch. They rode up just before pa left."

"I see."

She suddenly smiled, and Spur liked what it did to her appearance.

"I haven't even thanked you for saving my life! Why, I would have burned up like a cricket on the hearth if you hadn't helped me."

"It's nothing."

Their gazes met. Her wet lips parted. The woman stared steadily into his eyes, not smiling, not frowning, simply staring.

The moment passed. Patti tossed her head and laughed. "Oh, I must look a sight!" She tugged at her rumpled, smoke-blackened dress.

"Your garment is pretty well charred on the back," McCoy said.

"Then I guess I'd better take it off." She turned and closed her hotel room door. "Mister—mister what? What did you say your name was?"

"Spur McCoy."

"I see. Mr. McCoy, could you—"

"Turn my back? Of course." He started to move but the girl grabbed his wrists.

"No!" She grinned. "That wasn't what I was going to ask. Would you help me out of this old thing?"

He laughed and held her arms over her head. Spur gripped the waist of her shapeless dress and tugged it upward as he seemed to sink into her violet eyes.

The dress slipped past her face. It seemed to catch on something so he pulled harder and finally yanked it over whatever had impeded its purpose. Spur smiled as the woman's breasts popped past its hemline.

"My, my, Patti! You are a woman!"

"Told you, silly." She wiped her eyes and nose again and stepped back.

Spur took in the sight.

Her body was as white as lily petals save for the shocking pink tips of her breasts and the rich black fur that covered her mound. The swell of her hips, her slender waist and the oversized mounds of flesh that jutted from her torso made Spur comically pant.

Patti giggled again. "What are you waiting for?" she asked him.

"Uh, yeah, what *am* I waiting for?"

He jumped her. Patti dissolved into laughter as Spur caught her in his arms and carried her to the bed. Fortunately the small fire had spared it.

Nestled atop the comforter, Patti quickly undressed him, yanking at his vest, fumbling with the buttons that ran along his shirt front. Her hands were all over him.

"Maybe I should have taken 'em off before we got into bed," he said as his shirt parted, revealing his hairy torso.

"No. I like helping."

She slapped his rear and kneaded Spur's cheeks. Grinding his crotch against hers, feeling the excitement building in his body, McCoy twisted sideways, unbuttoned his pants and shoved them down.

"Let me help you!" Patti said.

She tugged on his pants legs. Their combined efforts finally produced the desired effect, and Spur pressed his naked body against hers.

"Oh, Spur!" Patti said. "Whatever is that I feel pressing against my naughty parts?"

He pretended to pull away from her. "If I have to tell you, you aren't a woman. Yet."

She squealed and grabbed his hips, slamming him down on top of her again. Patti groaned at his full weight. "Okay, okay. I was just playing."

"Yeah."

Spur bent his head and stuffed Patti's right nipple between his lips. It responded to his attention, stiffening and swelling. He gently teethed the delicious knob of flesh as the young woman slid her tongue into his ear.

"Ah!" she said.

The taste and the round fullness of Patti's breast made Spur switch to its twin sister. She writhed on the bed at the heat of his mouth, at the urgency of his sudden sexual arousal.

"God. Oh my god! Yes!"

He worked a hand between their groins and fingered Patti's outer lips. The woman wrapped her thighs around his and bucked. Spur's erection pressed against her stomach. His finger found the most delicate spot of her body.

Patti moaned. Spur rubbed harder. The young woman gasped and forced him from her groin.

They looked at each other with undisguised lust. Their breath met as it blasted from their mouths. Patti's eyes smouldered. Her lips quivered.

"I got another fire," she said.

"There?" He gently pinched her.

"Ah yes! Oh yes, Spur!"

He rubbed her clitoris as hard as he could without hurting her. "Want me to put it out?"

Patti nodded. "Yes. You can try, sir. It'll be quite a chore but you can try!"

He slipped out his hand. She stuffed a pillow under her buttocks. Their bodies fit together.

Spur slid into her.

His penis shook at her genital heat. Staring down at her lovely face, he hit bottom and withdrew.

The wideness of her eyes told him that she'd never had a man quite as large as him. Patti winced. Her anguished expression quickly melted into a satisfied leer.

The ageless magic swept them up. McCoy pumped, pushing into her mystery. Patti clamped her arms around his waist. Fingers dug into the flesh of his lower back. She urged him to do it with every nerve in her body.

"Jesus, Patti!" Spur said.

"Faster. Just do it faster!"

She bit her lip as he obeyed her command. Spur slammed into her. Their pubic bones crashed together, making the mattress lurch back and forth and up and down as they consummated their instant lust.

She was so young, so warm and willing that Spur didn't even try to hold back. He quickened his thrusts. The room filled with the scent of her musk and the sound of their moist bodies slapping against each other.

Patti sighed, arched on the bed and shook her head as she rocked through her pleasure. Spur groaned at the unstoppable sensations boiling up inside him.

"Higher. Harder!"

Spur lifted himself onto his hands and pounded into her. The new position increased her stimulation. Patti gasped. Open-mouthed, unblinking, the woman drank in the sight of the man above her and shuddered through another orgasm.

She didn't scream or cry out, but the woman's contractions around him told Spur everything he needed to know. She grabbed his shoulders and pulled him to her.

McCoy jammed his tongue into Patti's liquid mouth. His lips pistoned. The bed shook. Spur's testicles exploded. Her body milked his. McCoy rolled and gasped through his ecstasy, sucking her wet tongue, powerfully thrusting as he planted his seed into her willing body.

Patti O'Brannigan grabbed his buttocks, trying to force his orgasming erection deeper within her. Her lust increased the intensity of the moment. Spur's release seemed to stretch out, urged on by the young woman's mutual pleasure.

He pumped her until he could pump no more and collapsed on her moist body, spent, panting. He closed his eyes as every muscle in his body popped and relaxed.

They lay entangled together for a timeless moment. Spur's harsh breath mirrored the woman's. She clutched his biceps and moaned.

He dozed.

Patti's tongue on his bristly cheek roused him from his trance. The woman delicately licked the short, coarse hairs that had pushed through his face. Spur chuckled at the wet sensation and turned his head.

"Hello, ma'am."

"Hi yourself."

Their tongues met for an instant before he pulled away.

"Is it out?"

"What?" she said. "The cat?"

"The fire!"

Patti sighed and ran her hand through the damp hair. "I guess so. For now."

"Good. Always enjoy helping out a lady."

"Mmmmmm."

Their bodies were still connected. McCoy felt himself throbbing within the young woman's body.

"Ah, Patti?" he said.

"Hmmmmm?"

"Do you think we could set another fire?"

Patti smiled.

CHAPTER EIGHT

"Hey!" she yelled again from beside the fire. The nighttime desert air chilled her.

Burt Buxton pushed his hat lower over his face.

"I'm talking to you!" she said.

He sighed. The woman had been fun for a few minutes, but she was already holding him back, tying him down. He worked alone. He always had and always would.

"What is it, Kitty?" Buxton said into his hat.

"What do you think?" she demanded.

He lifted his hat. "I'm still not too happy with you. After all, you messed up a sure thing for me back in the Deadridge Bank."

Fully dressed in men's clothing again, the young woman got to her feet, put a hand on her hip and walked to their horse. "Oh my; I am so sorry. If I'd known, I would have checked your social calendar beforehand."

Burt Buxton grunted. In spite of himself, he was amused by the woman. "Alright, Kitty, alright."

Kitty Carson ran a finger through her flowing brown hair. "Well?"

"Well what?"

"Are you just going to stand there or are you going to help me?"

"Do what?" Burt yelled.

"Help me up on that dern beast of yours!"

Buxton sighed. "Whatever for? I told you we were out of danger. We can wait until first light to start moving again. You have a sudden hankering for a night-time ride?"

Kitty ruefully rubbed her rump. "Not much of one. Thanks to you I'll be sore for at least a week. It hurts like Hades! But I'm not going to stay here all night. I've got to get back to town."

Buxton stood. "Back to town? Are you serious?"

She smiled. "After all, that rifle-toting bank employee saw two men in his bank—but not a woman. I'm gonna be on the morning train out of Deadridge."

Burt grabbed her wrists. "You are not!"

"Try me." She grinned.

"I can't trust you! Hell, you'd probably tell the first lawman you see everything about me. You're not going anywhere tonight, Kitty Carson! Nowhere!"

She went limp in his hands. "Okay. Okay! Just let me loose! You know I can't get up onto that monstrous horse without your help!"

He searched her face and released her wrists.

The woman fingered the indentations his powerful hands had made in her soft flesh. "Great! Now two parts of me hurt."

"Make that four," Buxton said. He returned to his bedroll and stretched out. "Get some sleep, Kitty. I know I need it. We'll figure out what to do in the morning." He turned his back to her.

"Women!" he said, cursing the girl who'd ruined his latest bank robbery. He couldn't live without them, but they'd always complicated his life.

Buxton glanced over his shoulder at her. Kitty Carson smiled and walked to him. Before Burt knew what was happening her hand slid to the holster that was strapped to her right thigh and she drew her revolver.

He sat upright and held up his hands. "Make it a clear shot. Right through the heart."

She blinked.

"Come on, Kitty. You aren't going to use that thing. You're a woman!"

"And a woman can't or won't shoot?" She aimed. "Even you may have been able to figure out by now that I'm no delicate flower."

He stared hard at her.

"Sorry, Burt. I can't stay here with you—as much as I enjoyed tangling with you on the sand. I've got much better places to go out west."

"Banks?" he asked with a laugh.

"Guess again." Kitty pushed her boot into the left stirrup.

"Ah, ah, stores?"

"Uh-uh." She gripped the saddlehorn with a shaking hand. "Try once more."

Buxton started to stand, but she waved him back down. "You stay put!"

"I thought you couldn't mount up without my help!" he protested.

"That's what I said. You men always fall for my helpless-little-woman act." Kitty laughed and swung onto the saddle. She did it with surprising ease. She sweetened her aim as her delicious bottom hit the leather seat. "Don't try anything, Burt. Just let me go. I won't say a word about you."

"Maybe," Buxton said as he rose to his knees. "But how am I supposed to get out of here?"

"No one saw our faces," Kitty said. The beast pranced beneath her in confusion at the unfamiliar rider. "Just walk on back to town and start over."

"Hold on a minute!" Buxton said. "I don't take orders from anyone—man or woman!"

She kicked the mare's flanks. It hesitated. Kitty tried again, flicking the horse's reins. The beast reluctantly moved forward.

Buxton leapt to his feet and sped across the sand. "No you don't, you feisty wench!"

"What?"

He grabbed the woman's waist and physically pulled her from the saddle. Kitty Carson slid sideways into his waiting arms, kicking and clawing at his hands as the horse stopped to munch on a tasty, moonlit shrub.

"Let me go!" she screamed.

"No!"

He spun as she wildly shifted her weight. She

was all arms and legs and soft, warm bottom.
Her hair flew into his face; he spluttered and
got a better grip. The woman was as slippery
as a sack full of eels.

"I'll be, you're a horse-thief to boot!" Burt
said. "And I thought you were a lady!"

"Put me down this instant, Burt!" she
screamed into his ear.

"What'll I get if I do?"

"I won't tell."

Burt Buxton laughed and set her down.

"Some men have all the nerve!" Kitty said
as she looked up at him. "You think you own
me? Just because you picked a lousy night for
a bank robbery?"

He smiled. "Kitty!"

"What?"

Her face was soft in the diffused light. The
brown haired woman's rage visibly increased
her wild beauty. Buxton felt his pants tighten
at his crotch. "Get out of those man-clothes
again."

The young woman gasped.

Elijah Martin flung open the barn door,
flushed with the ride back from Deadridge and
the night's activities.

"Couldn't we sleep in the ranchhouse this
morning? Just this once?"

Fred Hardwick slapped his back. "Fuck no!"

Elijah frowned. "Ah jeez! After everything
that's happened? I feel like celebrating."

"I said no, boy. I meant it."

Elijah pouted and took off his hat. "Okay. I
guess you gave your word to that old man who
was here that we'd stay in the barn. But—"

Hardwick sat at the rickety table and brushed away the hay he'd piled on top of it. The mirror came into view. He propped the round, wooden-framed looking glass against a post behind the table and lit a lamp.

He had done his magic again. The whore had never suspected that he was an albino.

Fred wiped off the dark-hued facial cream. He grinned into the mirror as his natural, bone-white coloring showed through the cosmetic. The contrast was striking. "Did you like it, boy?" he asked as he worked. "Did you like pumping her?"

"Hell yes! That was some kind of fun!" Elijah dropped onto the bed of straw he'd made for himself. "And she really liked it too. Didn't she?"

Hardwick laughed. "She sure liked my money." The kid was so stupid, so innocent, he thought. But he'd come around. He'd learn that women were necessary evils, and that some of them could be bought and sold like horses in the untamed west.

"But she moaned and everything! When I was—you know—putting it in her!" Elijah scratched his head. "It sure *sounded* like she was enjoying it and everything."

"Then she fooled you. You weren't exactly her first man," Hardwick pointed out. "Maybe that night's first man, but the woman had done it before."

The youth put his hands behind his skull. "Oh. How come you wanted to watch, Mr. Holton?"

Hardwick laughed and continued scraping the cream off his face.

"No, really, Mr. Holton. And how come she had to be so ugly? Some of those gals in the saloon were real lookers! Big titties, big asses and everything!"

Hardwick sighed and chose another rag from the pile beside the table. "So you wouldn't fall for her, boy. Her being your first woman and all, it wouldn't be right. Besides, we'll be on the move soon."

"I know, I know!" Elijah rubbed his crotch. "Anyway, I had fun. I guess you did too— watching."

Hardwick slowed his wiping hand.

"You liked it more than me," Elijah continued.

Silence.

"Didn't you?"

Fancy Freddie Hardwick sighed. "Get some sleep, boy. We'll talk about it in the morning."

Elijah rolled over and buried his face in the straw. Sure they would. The bastard never talked about anything 'cept what he wanted to talk about.

He thought of the money he'd received from Hardwick for the jobs he'd gone on with his employer. Near to a hundred dollars! It wouldn't be long before he'd leave the freak behind and get him a real woman.

A beautiful woman.

And he'd do it to her without a white-faced outlaw staring at him, hooting and hollering as her body locked with his and he put it in her.

Patti O'Brannigan's lips parted as she slept. Spur drowsed beside her, smelling the stale odor of smoke. Meeting the woman had been interesting, but he had to take out a few minutes to do some thinking.

He shook his head until he was fully awake and pulled the blankets higher onto their bodies.

There must be someone else in town. Some man—make that man and woman—who'd tried to rob the bank.

He hadn't been able to follow the suspects due to an unfortunate set of circumstances. He didn't have much to go on but Spur hoped it would lead him to the responsible persons.

The population of Deadridge had swelled due to the temporary influx of passengers from the damaged train, he mused. Could there have been a thief or two on it? Someone who'd accidentally found himself in town with some time to pass?

The robberies did fit the ones that his boss had told him about. They'd been done at night. The safe had almost been opened without signs of violence. That could only be accomplished by an expert.

Ames had said his safe's dial had been left on the first number. The man was good.

Patti O'Brannigan rolled over. A hand touched his hairy chest. Spur sighed, pulled the woman closer to his body and closed his eyes.

Sleep, he told himself.

Millions of stars stared back at Kitty as the sweating man stopped moving on top of her. She'd enjoyed it almost as much as the first time, but it was getting cold.

"Burt?"

"Huh?"

"I have a problem," she said.

He grunted. "Yes, darling?"

"What am I going to do with you?"

"I think you just did it." He bit her ear.

"Hey! That's not what I'm talking about." She shivered in the wind that swept across the desert floor.

"I know. I was wondering the same thing myself, Kitty." He furrowed his brows. "Come on, that's not your real name. What is it?"

Kitty smiled. "I'm not telling."

"Hrmmmph. You don't trust me."

"No more than you trust me, darling."

"Hrmmmph."

She stared at the moon as it arced above them. "I guess there's only one solution."

"What's that?" His tongue found her ear.

"Since you won't let me go, I guess I'm your new partner."

His tongue quickly lost her ear. "What?"

"Come on, Burt. It won't be so bad. I've robbed banks before. I'm a pretty good shot. I can dress like a man so I won't attract much attention—at least while we're doing our work."

"Our work? *Our* work?"

"Calm down!" Kitty shook her head. "It sounds perfect to me. Where were you going next? After Deadridge, I mean?"

"I—" He pushed his head next to hers. "Very clever, young lady, but I'm not telling you. You'd probably find a way to leave me here all tied up and go off to do it yourself. Nothing doing!" He kissed her chin.

"Tied up?" Kitty smiled. "Dear, if anyone's going to be tied up it's me."

"What?"

"Oh, I've been known to enjoy that."

Buxton laughed and pressed his face between her breasts. "You drive a hard bargain, Kitty. A very hard bargain."

Something slithered across the sand. "Burt, ah, there's—there's—"

"Mmmmm?"

She grasped his head and lifted it. "Look!"

He moved swiftly, smashing the rattlesnake's skull with a rock before it could begin to think about spreading around its venom.

"See? We make a good team." Kitty Carson laughed.

CHAPTER NINE

In the morning, Spur took his leave of the young woman whom he'd saved from the flames, ate a hearty breakfast in the Deluxe Hotel dining room and went to the only livery stable in town. He hired himself a fine roan gelding, paid for a week in advance, and tied her up at a hitching post in the middle of town.

He wanted to make sure that he wouldn't lack a mount again. That done, he started looking.

Spur stopped by the Red Garter saloon. It was fairly empty at 6:30 A.M., but he knew he had to talk to the saloon girls in town. One of them might have seen Fred Hardwick.

A sad-eyed whore, who was even less attractive than most working women on the frontier, raised a sleepy smile at him and staggered over to the bar as McCoy paid for a whiskey.

"Howdy," she said.

Spur tipped his hat and took his drink. "Come to my table?" he asked her.

"Sure."

The whore stifled a yawn as they sat in the rear of the Red Garter. Spur took a sip and looked evenly at her. "You had many customers lately?"

The saloon girl rolled her eyes and slumped. "Oh hell! You're one of those talkers, ain't ya?"

"Yes, I am. I'm looking for a man."

"Aren't we all!" Her cheek rested on a puddle on the surface of the table. "Which one?"

"A man by the name of Fred Hardwick, or Fancy Freddie Hardwick."

"Never heard of him." She closed her eyes. "Wait a minute. Fancy Freddie?"

"Yes." Did she know something?

"Heck, I'm still asleep. I was wrong. Sure I've seen him!" She didn't open her eyes.

The woman had had far too much liquor and no sleep, from the looks of her. Spur gently tilted back her head.

"Where?"

"Here. Right here." Her eyes wandered. She couldn't seem to focus.

"In Deadridge?"

"Yeah."

"Woman, I need you to tell me everything you know about this Fancy Freddie Hardwick. How long ago was this? Yesterday? The day before?"

"Hell no!" she blared. "It must've been two years ago."

McCoy shook his head. "I don't understand."

The whore smiled up at him and winked. "I

saw him in the post office. On the wall. In a picture." She hiccuped. "Yeah. I make it a point to remember outlaws' faces so I can spot them. I like the reward money."

Spur nodded. It figured. "Then you've never seen him in the flesh?"

"Nope. Heard he got strung up somewhere. That's why his picture ain't there no more." Her cheek dropped to the table again. The saloon girl gripped the edge of the filthy surface and popped her lips.

"So you haven't seen any albinos in town."

"Those white freaks? No. But I had a strange customer last night—two of them."

"Yeah?"

"Well, this tall guy brings in this young buck and has me pop his cherry." She licked her lips. "Only, see, the tall guy watched what we did. He liked it—watching, that is."

Spur nodded.

"Funny thing about it was, it looked like the tall guy had some kind of makeup on."

He stretched. "Makeup?" He thought about the perfume he'd smelled in the bank. "You mean rouge? Eyeliner? Lipstick?"

"Naw, naw, naw. Almost looked like he'd put some dark cream all over his face. You know? To make it look like he'd been out in the sun."

Spur took the whore's hand, but she pulled away from him. "Ma'am, I—"

"Ma'am! Ma'am?" she laughed and wearily lifted her head. "How long's it been since I heard anyone call me that? Everyone knows me as Squirrel-Faced Sally."

"Sally, what color were his eyes?"

Her head rolled unsteadily on her neck. "I

don't know. It was too dark in my room to tell, and he never got real close—at least, while I could see him."

It could be Hardwick, Spur thought. That could be why no one had noticed him in town. His appearance on the street had been so quick that he could have left before anyone had spotted him. But the rest of the time he must have worn some kind of makeup to hide his obvious appearance.

It made sense. If he kept his hat brim down low his pink eyes wouldn't be so obvious.

"Sally."

The whore's head hit the table. She softly moaned.

McCoy shook her. "Squirrel Face, did he say where he was staying?"

She yawned and rubbed her eyes with a whiskey-wetted finger. "Nope. Didn't do much talking 'cept to tell that boy to do it harder to me. Not as if it lasted very long, anyway." She hiccuped again and the visible half of her lips creased into a smile.

"Thanks, Sally. I'm at the Deluxe Hotel, Room 12. If you see him again I'd be mighty obliged if you'd come tell me." He thrust a silver dollar into the woman's hand.

The cold metal around her fingers woke her. Sally sat up and grinned at him. "Sure, sure, boy. But I gotta get me some shut-eye."

He walked away as the unattractive whore slipped into unconsciousness. The coin fell from her hand.

A half-hour later the train pulled in right on schedule. Spur stood nearby, watching the boarding passengers. He waved at Engineer

Taggert, but the man was far too busy to speak to him as he supervised the complicated operation and yelled at the train's conductor.

Could one or more of the passengers have been responsible for the attempted robbery of the Deadridge Bank? Could Fred Hardwick have been on the train, or could he be boarding now?

McCoy searched every face, watched every man, woman and child who climbed onto the train. He saw no one who even slightly resembled the albino outlaw.

He cursed and shoved his boot toe into the sand.

Kitty Carson grabbed Burt Buxton's sleeve as they walked out of the Deluxe Hotel. She'd washed and changed into her regular female traveling clothes—a simple grey skirt and white blouse with a bonnet and gloves.

The train sat at the station right where's she'd hoped it would be. Steam rose from its great stack as a crowd of people anxiously boarded it.

"Wait!" she said. "You sure no one can recognize us? I mean from last night?" she whispered into Buxton's ear.

He nodded. "Now, now, Kitty. We've been over this. There's no way anyone could. It was too dark. The man in the bank certainly never saw our faces. Not one lamp was lit! Ease your mind."

"Sure. Oh sure!"

Buxton scowled at her. "This is the kind of partner you're going to be? A scared little girl?"

"I'm not a little girl, Burt. You know that!"

"Perhaps not in some things."

Kitty stared at the train. "I can't get onto that thing. Not yet. Not today."

He sighed. "I thought we had a deal. You go with me and we split the profits."

"I know, but—"

"Last night you said you couldn't wait to leave Deadridge. What's changed your mind?"

Kitty licked her lips and put down her bag. "I don't know. But I'm not going. You can if you want. I won't try to stop you." She extended a gloved finger. "Go, my good man. Leave me here all alone!"

Buxton grinned. "Nothing doing, little lady. You're coming with me!"

He clutched her hand and wrenched the woman toward the train.

"Wait! My bag!" Kitty said.

"I can buy you anything you want!"

She kicked his ankle. He howled and let her go. The woman raced back to retrieve her bag.

"You brute!" she said. A whistle pierced the air. "Get on your train. It's leaving!"

"All aboard!" the conductor yelled.

"Not so fast!" Burt Buxton went to the woman and put his arm around her shoulder. "Kitty, I'm rich. I'll pay you good money to travel with me. How about it? I'll give you more than you could ever pull out of some little safe somewhere—if you really know how to do that man's work."

She stiffened in his arm. "Unhand me, sir! We are in public!"

He propelled the protesting woman toward the train. "No. Make up your mind—you're coming with me."

A tall, handsome man stood nearby, watching the passengers boarding the train. He seemed the type of gentleman who'd help a lady in distress. Kitty tightened her throat. She screamed.

The stranger rushed up to them. His reddish-brown moustache twitched. "What are you doing?" he barked at Buxton.

"It's nothing," Burt said, smoothing on a smile. "My wife's just scared of trains. That's all. And the accident didn't help much."

The stranger seemed to take it all in. My god, was he believing Burt?

Kitty struggled harder. "I'm not his wife! He's trying to kidnap me!"

The man easily knocked apart the two of them. A second whistle blasted into the morning air. The conductor stepped up on the passenger car. Burt Buxton sneered at the man who'd helped Kitty Carson.

"If you're going to be on that train, be on it now," the stranger said.

He nodded, shot a look at Kitty and ran for it.

Buxton raced up the steps and stepped up to the train as the car started to roll forward.

"Are you alright?" the stranger asked the woman.

Kitty put down her bag again, rubbed her wrists and nodded. "Yes. I'm fine. Thanks to you."

He tipped his hat and grinned. "Spur McCoy, at your service."

She was a pretty young woman, McCoy instantly decided, as she stood before him. She glanced at the train and watched her attacker staring at them through a window.

The great engine roared. Its iron wheels turned. The train slowly pulled away from the Deadridge station.

"I don't know what went on between you two," Spur said as he turned back to the woman. "That's not my business. As long as you're safe I'll leave you alone."

The woman extended her hand. "Kitty Carson, sir."

He smiled at the name and took her hand. The woman had a surprisingly hard grip. She seemed to change before his eyes. Her bosom rose. Her chin tilted upward. She smiled and widened her emerald eyes.

"Normally I can take care of myself," Kitty said. "But that man tricked me!"

Spur looked down at her traveling bag. "But you were planning to leave?"

"Well yes. But not with him! When I knew he was going to be on the train I quickly changed my mind."

"I see." He didn't, of course, but there was nothing unusual about that when it came to women.

Kitty sighed. "Now that that's over, I might as well tell you the truth." She moved closer to him. "I met him last night and he was so nice. Then, this morning, he announced that we were leaving together. I was just pretending to go with him. He and I had a, well, a good time until early this morning."

Not a trace of color entered her cheeks. Spur nodded.

"He got this wild idea that I was gonna

marry him and have his babies! I put a stop
to that—with your help, I mean. I can't thank
you enough."

"No problem," Spur said.

Kitty looked him up and down. "I can trust
you, can't I?"

"Sure."

She glanced around the street. "Is there
somewhere we can go? Just to talk, I mean.
Somewhere private?"

"Of course."

Spur soon closed his hotel room's door and
turned to the woman who stood in the center
of the floor clutching her leather bag.

Kitty Carson turned to him and smiled, but
her mirth quickly faded. The woman rubbed
her forehead. "What a morning! I've hated this
town ever since I've seen it."

"You've been through a lot, from what
you've said. I was there during the train
accident."

The beautiful woman shook her head. "I'm
not going to think about that. I won't!"

"Okay. Why don't you say what's on your
mind?"

Kitty frowned. "I know I should tell this to
the sheriff, but there isn't one here. No
marshall either, from what I've gathered."

"That's correct," he said.

Kitty bit her lower lip. "It's kind of difficult
to say, but I just have to tell someone!"

"Please, sit down." Spur nodded to the single
chair.

The woman slipped into it and placed her
bag on the floor. She tugged at her skirt. "That
man you just saved me from? The one who

jumped onto the train?"

Spur nodded.

"He scared me. I mean, I was afraid for my very life just being near him!"

"But you spent the night—I mean, you *talked* with him until morning?"

"That's right."

McCoy put out his hands. "Why were you scared?"

She lowered her voice. "He's a thief. He tried to rob the Deadridge Bank last night."

CHAPTER TEN

"What?" Spur grunted and dashed to the door. "That was the man who tried to rob the Deadridge Bank?"

"Wait!" Kitty shouted and stood.

"Why?"

"You can't catch him. We both saw him get on the train just as it was leaving. He's long gone by now, Spur."

He set his jaw. "Then I'll follow it."

She laughed. "On horseback? You'd never make it. It must be a hundred miles until the next stop. Never mind about him; he's out of my hair now."

Spur looked at her, panted, and nodded.

Kitty studied his face. "My, you sure are interested in him. You have a personal stake? Maybe got some money in the bank or something?"

"No, no." Spur silently cursed. He'd had his hands on the thief responsible for the robberies. He'd had him! And he'd let him get away.

Kitty stared at him. "Well, you sure aren't happy to see him leave. But at least this way he won't be trying it again. Not here, anyway."

"He's done others, right?" Spur asked the woman. "He's robbed other banks?"

She nodded. "Yes. From what I gather this was his seventh or eighth robbery—at least, it was supposed to be. You're wondering how I know all this?" She made a face. "Because he made me watch him do it last night! The bastard said if I didn't go with him he'd shoot me!"

Spur walked over to her and pushed his nose into her hair.

"Hey! Not that I'm complaining, but what are you doing?" she asked with a laugh.

The perfume that rose from her neck and shoulders matched the scent that had permeated the Deadridge Bank. At least she was telling the truth about that. "Just checking something." He patted her hand.

"Anyway, Burt's long gone and I'll never have to worry about him again." Kitty smiled and returned to her chair, but the expression on Spur's face made her frown. "Hey, what is all this? How come you're so—"

"Kitty, I'm a lawman."

She lifted an eyebrow. "Really?"

"Yes. I'm investigating a string of bank robberies that have occurred in Arizona and California during the last few months. The only reason I'm here in Deadridge is because of the train accident."

"Me too." She touched her breastbone. "Why, no wonder you're so upset! Spur, if I'd known you were a lawman I wouldn't have let Burt Buxton get away! I hope you believe me!"

"Of course I do," he wearily said.

"What happens now?"

Spur shrugged. "I don't know." He knelt beside her. "Kitty, you don't know any albinos, do you?"

It had been a hard fall. He'd tried to roll through it on his shoulder, but the ground had smacked into his body with the force of a thousand fists. Now that he'd finally come to a rest the man kept still, staring at the brilliant sky overhead, waiting for the tremendous pounding in his shoulder to ease before he moved.

A ragged bird flew far above him, riding the heat that rose from the desert floor. Its graceful arcs were hypnotic. His eyelids closed. He dozed.

Two hours later he awoke. His face was scorched. Thirst had transformed his mouth into a fiery desert of its own. His whole body seemed to ache, and the sand burned through his fine clothing.

Have to get up, he told himself. Have to stand up and find some shade.

Have to!

He lifted his head, shook it and blinked. Planting his hands on either side of his body, he pushed against the sand and lifted his torso.

Burt Buxton sat up.

The train tracks stretched for miles before him. Just behind, not more than two miles distant, lay Deadridge. Its buildings seemed to emerge from a shimmering lake.

Mirage, he told himself.

Not water.

Not real.

Driven by thirst, confused by the blow he'd received when he'd leaped from the steaming train, Burt Buxton stood, found his hat, stuffed it onto his head and started back to town.

He reeled around. No. Not right. Kitty was there. Kitty'd spread the word about him. She was just that kind of woman. Where else could he go?

He lowered the brim of his fine hat to shield his eyes from the glare and circled. Buildings sprouted a mile or so outside of town. To the southwest.

Buxton brushed off his suit and walked toward the desolate ranch.

An hour later his ankles ached from the pain of thrusting them into the sand and wrenching them free again. The endless cycle had left him exhausted. His last reserves of energy were gone by the time he collapsed against a barn wall and sank into the blessed shadow cast by the sun.

Water, he told himself.

After a short rest, Buxton crawled to a nearby pump. His arm refused to function at first but he perservered. The sand-blasted handle finally went up and down. A tantalizing dribble spurted from the spout. Buxton licked it and pumped. He sighed as chilled water, forced from far beneath the ground, splattered all over his face.

The thief stopped drinking and crawled to the shade.

No one had challenged him at the pump, he thought. Where were the ranch's owners?

"Keep close," Hardwick said to the wild-eyed youth as they rode into Deadridge.

"Yes, Mr. Holton."

"We're gonna put the fear of God into that damned bastard who tried to have me hanged." Hardwick smiled as they passed the first few buildings. This was going to be fun. He was looking forward to scaring McCoy.

They left their mounts at the closest hitching post. Hardwick affected his stiff-legged walk and stoop. The position of his head lowered his hat, making it difficult for anyone to look into his eyes. He hoped the desert sun wouldn't melt off the cream that he'd used to cover his face. It had worked so poorly on his hands, during the day at least, that he'd taken to wearing gloves. They worked, and that was all that was necessary.

"What's he look like?" Elijah asked with a plaintive glance at the saloon where he'd lost his virginity.

"I'll tell you later. Don't look around or anything. Don't act suspicious. Just walk!"

"Yes, boss."

Fred Hardwick grinned below his hat. He hadn't planned his second attack on McCoy. It was more fun to make it up as he went along. He assumed that the man hadn't left town on the train that morning. Hardwick didn't see

McCoy as the kind who'd turn his tail and run.

"Follow me, boy!" he said, slipping into an alley.

Elijah followed him.

"What do we do now?"

"We wait, kid. We wait for him to show his ugly face." Hardwick spat.

Elijah nodded. "Okay. And then, after it's over, maybe the saloon again?"

Hardwick looked at his young companion. "You're worse than a rabbit, Elijah!"

The boy blushed. "What about it? Can I? Huh? Please, Mr. Holton?"

Fancy Freddie shrugged. "We'll see how well you do on this assignment."

Elijah nodded and touched his holster. "All loaded up and ready to go!"

"Remember. Don't kill him, if at all possible. That's my job, and I'll wait it out a while."

The youth nodded.

Kitty Carson's surprising revelation about this Burt Buxton hadn't made Spur's morning. He'd worked on plenty of cases like this but never one that was so convoluted, so full of annoying surprises.

He went to the telegraph office and found it locked up. A short message stated that the lines were still down. Repairs should be finished soon. It was signed, "One-Eyed Jack."

McCoy grunted. So he'd have to leave General Halleck in the dark for a few days. Buxton might be gone, but Hardwick was still in town. He'd concentrate on finding him for the time being.

He walked down the street, breathing dust,

sweating under his heavy clothing. Hot lead buried itself into the sand near his feet. Spur stopped. No shots followed it.

Hardwick? he thought. Hardwick!

Spur searched the surrounded area, running up and down alleys, racing along streets, poking into saloons and stores.

Nothing. No sign of him. Not a goddamned trace!

He'd passed out again. The sound of approaching horses violently snapped Burt Buxton from his sleep. He stood, leaned heavily against the barn, and looked up as the men rode toward the ranch.

What kind of people were they? He only hoped they'd look favorably on a helpless man trapped in the desert.

They reined in their horses near the corral. The riders remained on their mounts. One, the taller of the two, didn't challenge him as he slid from his saddle and tied up the beast. The youth soon dismounted, glancing at the haggard man, and quickly set to rubbing down the two frothing horses.

The older man approached. "Howdy," he cautiously said, and lifted his head.

Buxton nearly collapsed in relief. "Hardwick? Hardwick! Fancy Freddie Hardwick!"

The boy quickly drew, but Hardwick raised a hand to stop him.

"Do I know you, sir?" the pink-eyed man said.

"No. But I sure as shit know about you! I heard you got away from that rope that had your name on it in St. Louis a couple years back." He smiled. "Oh, I'm Burt Buxton—at least, that's my name this week. Just got into town a few days ago."

"So?" Hardwick said. He crossed his arms.

Buxton winced. "So I was run out of town by a goddamned dame who interrupted me while I was breaking into the Deadridge Bank's safe last night. I jumped from the train and made my way here."

"You look like shit, Buxton," Hardwick grinned. "I heard about the bungled bank job that went up last night."

"That was me."

"I see. How'd you know I was here?"

"I didn't! It was the first place I could find water. I hope you don't mind, I took a sip or two."

"I don't give a damn about that."

Hardwick stared hard at the man. Burt's sun-fried brain knew that he was being summed up by a master. He tried to grin but his lips were cracked.

"Hey Buxton, you looking for a place to stay around here—out of town?"

"Sure!"

"You wanna work for me?"

Elijah's boots scuffed the dirt beside the horses.

Buxton tried to think. The man was known for his bloody hold-ups and bank robberies. But it was the best offer he'd had all day, and he wasn't feeling up to resisting.

"Work for you?" he scratched his blistered chin and winced in pain. "Why the hell wouldn't I? You're the best, Hardwick!"

The albino smiled. "That kind of talk'll make you go far, Buxton. Okay. We'll find you a place to bunk."

"That's it?" Burt asked, glancing back at the fuming youth. "You mean I can stay on with you?"

"Sure. For now. I'll fill you in on my operation later. Oh, and about this woman who ran you out of town?"

Buxton groaned.

"Woman!" Elijah said, dropping his brush. "Boss, you didn't take me to see my woman!"

Hardwick felt his pocket. "Yeah. And I saved myself two dollars."

CHAPTER ELEVEN

Two hours later, Buxton was feeling much better. The shaded barn was downright luxurious compared to the sun-dazzled desert that lay outside its doors.

He'd splashed cool water onto his face but that hadn't helped kill the pain of his sunburn.

"Damnit!" Buxton said. "My face is burning up!"

Hardwick snapped his fingers and took a blue-glassed jar from the rickety table.

"Rub some of that onto it," he said, tossing the container to Buxton.

He did. The sticky liquid soothed his face. The pain vanished.

"Don't ask me!" Hardwick said, lifting his hands. "I don't know what's in it, but it's worked more than once when I've taken a nap face-up in the sun."

"Thanks, Hardwick!"

"Call me Holton," Freddie said.

"Right."

"I've told you about the man I met up with here in town," Hardwick said.

The man dabbed more of the gooey liquid onto his face. "What was his name again?" He scratched his head. "I'm still a little dumb yet from the heat."

"You'll get used to it. His name, Buxton, is Spur McCoy. And he's my target. He'll never leave Deadridge alive."

Elijah raked away some soiled hay. "But you could have killed him in town today!" the boy said.

Hardwick turned to him. "That wouldn't have been fun, Elijah. You have to do these things correctly."

The youth shrugged and returned to his work.

Hardwick glanced into the mirror. He still hadn't wiped off his brown-tinted makeup but he loathed the unmanly job. "Aw fuck it!" he said.

"What? Fuck what?" Elijah asked.

Hardwick laughed. "Hell, boy; ever since you had your first woman you've been so horny you're ready to slide it into anything with two legs!"

"Of four, from the looks of him," Buxton said.

Hardwick roared. The boy blushed.

"When you planning on doing your next job?" the man asked the albino. "I'm not trying to crowd in on your territory, but a man does get to wondering.,"

"Sure, I understand," Hardwick bit off the tip of a cigar and lit it. "Two days, maybe three. I was planning on hitting the Deadridge Bank. Still may do it."

"Yeah? They'll be hiring on guards and watching it day and night. At least, they probably will. I nearly had its safe when that woman—" He shook his head.

"Like I keep telling young Elijah here, women can be fun but they're a damned pain in the ass."

"It ain't my ass that's hurting," the boy said as he rubbed his testicles.

Hardwick ignored him. "What's a few guards? You worry too much, Buxton. I got you, the kid and my man in town. That's four of us. That's more than enough of us to get the job done. Don't you think?"

Burt nodded. "Sure!"

Hardwick frowned. "I know you aren't the type of man who's afraid to spill some blood. It does become necessary in our line of work."

Buxton nodded. "I know. Haven't for quite a while, but money's money. I'll do whatever you tell me to do to get my share."

"Great! Buxton, I have the feeling we've got the beginning of a beautiful relationship going here."

He smiled. "The coffee ready yet?"

"Almost."

Hardwick lit his cheroot. "We'll wait a day or two. And meanwhile, I'll be thinking up ways to scare the bejesus out of Spur McCoy."

The woman who called herself Kitty Carson said she hadn't met any albinos during her brief stay in Deadridge, and Spur had no reason to doubt her.

But the rest of her story didn't quite pan out. He knew she was holding back something, but he had to gently question the woman.

A fine noon-meal made Spur feel better. Kitty had taken a room in the Deluxe and had made no sexual overtures to him as he'd left the woman to her beauty sleep. After the meal, Spur was making his way outside when the woman who'd been burning up last night stopped him with a word.

"Spur!"

He turned and tipped his hat. Patti O'Brannigan smiled as she descended the stairs.

"Care to accompany me on a walk?" she asked, unfurling her parasol.

"Why not?"

She took his arm.

They went outside. "Actually, I've decided to return to the ranch. As much as I enjoyed meeting you," Patti said with a blush, "I'm worried about it. My father's due back today or tomorrow anyway, so why shouldn't I just get on home?"

"How far is it from Deadridge?"

Patti shrugged. "Two miles at most. Not far."

He nodded. "Uh-huh. And how were you planning on getting your pretty little behind out there?"

"Spur!" she said in mock shock. "Me and my pretty little behind will be just fine, thank you. Paul up to the livery stable's been keeping my buggy and horse. I'll just get it and ride out there."

"Alone? Across the desert?" he asked.

"I do it once a month to stock up on things. Spur, I've lived here since I was a little girl. I can take care of myself." She patted his arm. "We're here."

They stopped before the livery stable where Spur had rented his horse. "I can't change your mind?"

She shook her head. "Sorry. I must be going. Paul!" she yelled over her shoulder.

The greasy-shirted, dumb-witted man appeared, wiping his hands on the leather apron that covered his bulky midsection.

"Yeah, Miss O'Brannigan?"

"Hitch Reggie to my buggy, will you?"

He burped. "Of course, Miss O'Brannigan."

Patti turned to Spur. Her eyes flickered amusedly. "I'll be fine. Really I will be."

"If you're sure, I'll leave you to it." Spur kissed her cheek. "I hope to see you again, Miss O'Brannigan."

"Same here, Mr. McCoy."

He snapped his fingers. "I just remembered! What about your room?"

Patti looked at the sky. "Oh, I'm sure they'll hold my things in lieu of payment. My father'll straighten it all out when he returns."

"Great. Have a safe journey, Miss O'Brannigan."

"Thanks. I will!"

He walked directly to the hitching post where he'd left his rented mount. The roan gelding knickered as Spur rubbed its head. "Boy," he said, "we're going on a ride. Just you and me—following that foolish girl."

The horse questioningly turned its huge brown eyes toward Spur.

It wasn't that he didn't trust her, McCoy told himself an hour later as he followed the buggy. He didn't trust the desert and the men who lived in it.

Patti's night-black conveyance was impossible to miss as it rolled across the desert. It moved so slowly that he walked beside his horse most of the time, cutting across the open terrain, veering past clumps of cottonwoods and stands of aged cactus to shield himself from her view.

He had no idea where to look for Hardwick anyway. Might as well make sure the little woman got home safely.

McCoy stopped a half hour later. The woman had pulled up the buggy to a ranchhouse. Nearby sat a well-constructed barn. A few horses frisked in the corral. Past the buildings Spur saw brown lumps littering a surprisingly green slope. A stream sparkled as it ran through the area. Cattle.

Spur moved closer. The woman stepped from the buggy. Three figures appeared from the barn. He saw signs of a struggle.

He stepped into the saddle and urged his horse to a run. The roan instantly obeyed. All four people had disappeared into the barn by the time Spur rode up to it.

McCoy dismounted and drew his Colt .44, wishing he'd brought his rifle. The barn doors were closed. He couldn't see inside, but he sure could hear.

"Tarnation, woman! You aren't supposed to

be back yet!" a man said.

"I—I just came back early! Heavens, Mr. Holton! You can stay on another night if you want! It certainly wouldn't put me out!"

"We can?"

"Of course! I'm not about to tell you and your friends to leave. And I won't disturb you. I promise!"

"Well . . ."

"It's just not right," a deeper voice said. "Having a woman out here."

"But it's my spread!" Patti said.

Someone laughed. "You run this place all by your lonesome? What about the old man, the one who told us we could stay here for a few days until he got back?"

"Okay, it's my father's and mine," Patti said. "I can come and go as I please. After all, Mr. Holton, you and your friends are my guests."

"Shut up!"

The other voice again.

Spur couldn't wait any longer. He stepped into the barn.

A tall man faced the woman, his arms crossed over his chest, head down. A youth stood nearby. Neither had drawn their weapons, and neither noticed him.

"Miss O'Brannigan?" Spur said.

The woman turned. "Spur!"

The older man stared up at him. Spur barely saw his eyes before his feet were kicked out from under him and he crashed onto the straw-covered floor.

"Take care of him!" the man yelled.

Someone jumped on top of him and slammed

a pillow onto his face. The soft, light sack turned into an instrument of death. Suffocating, Spur pounded his elbows into his attacker's midsection.

The man howled and stuffed the pillow harder against McCoy's mouth and nose. The feather-filled cloth cut off his air supply. He couldn't breathe.

Spur raised his knees and drove both boots into his assailant's chest. The sudden pressure knocked him backward. McCoy threw off the pillow and stood. The sun-burned man quickly knocked him to the dirt floor again.

The woman screamed. Spur was too busy fighting off the vicious bastard to pay much attention to her. The two men grappled, neither able to get a firm hold.

They rolled on the floor. The straw slicked their motion. Spur desperately tried to lay one good punch on the man but he twisted back and forth, tearing at McCoy's shirt front. He wasn't a good fighter but he was a slippery one.

Damnit, Spur thought. Hold still!

A fist bruised his right side. McCoy cursed as the man wriggled from his grip again and grabbed a nail-studded piece of wood.

Spur jerked his head to the right. Five rusty nails slammed into the earthen floor inches from his cheek.

The man stood over him.

"Jesus!" McCoy said aloud as he stood and got his first clear view of the man's face. It was the bank thief. The one he'd thought had left Deadridge on the train.

"Buxton!" he said. "This one's for Curly Ames!" Spur plowed a fist into his jaw.

The thief's knees buckled and shook. The big man crumpled to the ground.

Spur wiped his face and looked around. The dark-faced man, the boy and Patti were gone.

CHAPTER TWELVE

"Shit!" Spur yelled.

Burt Buxton, the would-be robber, groaned from the barn's earthen floor.

The Secret Service agent grabbed a piece of rope and quickly tied the barely conscious man's hands behind his back. He secured the thief to one of the six-inch thick posts that held up the hay loft.

"You move and you're dead meat!" McCoy said. He dashed outside.

There was no sign of the youth, or the taller man, or of Patti O'Brannigan.

The buggy sat just where Patti had left it. Spur's rented mount was still in place. A few other horses, still saddled, drank from a nearby trough.

Where the hell were they?

The ranchhouse. It was worth a try, Spur

thought as he dug his boots into the sandy soil and exploded toward it.

The back door stood open.

He stopped outside the threshold. It was silent inside the house. Spur stepped in.

"Shut up!"

The voice was soft. It came from upstairs.

McCoy went to the long, bent flight and tested the first step. It didn't creak, so he continued upward, step by step, grasping the rail in his left hand and the Colt .44 in his right.

Two gunshots made him recoil on the stairs. Spur took them three at a time as blue smoke and the smell of gunpowder boiled down into the stairwell.

Glass broke somewhere overhead. Spur followed the noise to a bedroom.

The young boy who'd been downstairs was sprawled on the floor. McCoy shook his head as he saw who was beside him—Patti O'Brannigan.

He knelt, glancing at the smashed second-story window. Patti stared up with umoving eyes. He checked both of their pulses; they were dead.

The man was a good shot. Spur gently laid a blanket over Patti's lifeless body. He stuck a leg through the window and jumped.

McCoy's rage numbed him. He barely felt himself hit the stack of firewood. It spilled him to the ground. On his feet again, Spur saw a distant figure mounting up. He cursed and ran for his horse. As he passed the barn, someone knocked him to the ground.

Buxton!

Hands clamped around Spur's neck, jerking

it back. He roared and dug his boot heel into his Buxton's toes.

"Damnit, Buxton!" Spur said. "I tied you up!"

"Didn't check to see if I had a knife in my boot!" the man roared. "Did you?"

Spur twisted around and slammed Buxton into the sand. The man howled. McCoy stood.

"I don't have time for you, Buxton!" Spur said, staring down at him. Blood oozed from his chin. He didn't look too good.

"That's what you think!" The thief grabbed McCoy's leg and pulled hard.

"Damnit, Buxton!" Spur kicked. "Your friend—the one who's getting away—just killed the boy and the woman."

The thief wouldn't release McCoy's leg. He spun around the man. "Yeah. He knows what he's doing, especially when it comes to killing. Old Hardwick's a mean bastard."

Hardwick.

"That wasn't the albino," Spur said as he tried to kick the man's face. "That wasn't Fancy Freddie Hardwick!" His foot jabbed the air on either side of Buxton's head.

"Hah! A lot you know. He's wearing something on his face to make him look just like us. And you never saw him up close. That was Fred Hardwick!"

The sole of Spur's boot connected with Buxton's face. The pressure around his ankle disappeared. The would-be bank robber slapped his hands onto his face as McCoy broke free.

"You bastard!" Blood oozed from between the downed man's fingers. "You tore up my face!"

"Sorry, Buxton. Guess the girls won't be falling all over themselves to grab your meat!" Spur looked up. Hardwick was nowhere in sight. "I oughta kill you right now."

Instead, he retrieved the man's knife from his boot, sliced through Buxton's clothing and stripped him to his longjohns. The man blubbered as he sat on the sand, still covering his face. Spur yanked off his boots.

"What—what are you doing?"

"This."

Spur dragged him to the front porch of the ranch house and tied him as securely as he could. "You aren't hiding a knife now!" he said as he ran to his mount.

They took off. The roan tore up the sand as Spur sped from the ranch. The soft granules hadn't left very clear tracks, but he soon found a trail of horse hoof impressions. They led into the rolling hills behind the ranch.

"Giddyup, boy!" Spur yelled.

The gelding reared back its head in response and put on full power.

Damnit, Spur thought. Both men he'd been looking for were in the same place. Hardwick's disguise had fooled him—and most of the residents of Deadridge as well. Spur remembered the saloon girl he'd talked to. Hardwick must have been the one wearing the makeup. And the young buck who'd lost his cherry now lay dead back at the ranch.

Beside him was Patti O'Brannigan, who hadn't been able to wait another day to return to her spread.

He topped a small rise. Hardwick wasn't in

sight beyond it, so Spur drove the horse down the gentle slope. It's hooves tore into the sand, obliterating the outlaw's tracks, creating new ones.

Where could Hardwick go? Spur frowned as he remembered what he'd learned about the man's plan of action. He moved into an area, studied it, found every hiding hole within four or five miles of it, then robbed the bank, murdering everyone who got in the way.

He could be headed anywhere. These rolling, wind-eroded cliffs weren't helping much. Though Spur was clearly still following Hardwick's trail he never spotted the rider.

His mount strained under the hot desert sun. Its skin shone. It whinneyed against the tremendous work that Spur was forcing it to do, but he pushed it on for another half-hour.

"Okay, boy," Spur said, and reined her in. He dismounted. Hoove tracks were splattered across the sand, leading directly away from him. And just up ahead . . . .

Spur wiped his forehead and went forward ten feet. Another set of tracks, leading toward him, appeared beside the first. They quickly veered off, disappearing into some waist-high brush that didn't seem to have been recently trampled.

What in hell was going on?

He squatted. The tracks seemed to have been made by the same horse, but the soft sand made it impossible to see the subtle variations in the hoof prints. As Spur bent lower he noticed something he hadn't seen during his hasty ride. Yellow dust blew across the tracks that led away from him into the hills.

It must be some kind of pollen, he thought, nodding. But a quick search of the area showed no flowering cacti, no plants that could have created it.

The breeze must have carried it. Spur took off his hat and thought longingly of his canteen. He returned to his mount, poured some of the water into his hat and let the horse drink as he swallowed a few precious drops.

The tracks he was following might be a blind. Hardwick was such a damned clever man that he could have made them earlier that morning, leading in a false direction, just in case he had some problems out at the ranch.

It was possible. Hardwick couldn't have had more than a four minute lead on him. He couldn't have ridden a mile or two and swung back this close. He simply hadn't had the the time.

Then where was he?

"HARDWICK!" Spur yelled.

The word echoed through the brownish-red cliffs, bouncing off endless sheer walls. It disturbed a mass of white butterflies into sudden flight. McCoy roared again but the only sound that answered him was his own voice.

His horse finished drinking. It's long tongue lapped at the drops of water that glistened from its lips. Spur returned his sodden but cooler hat to his head and rode back to the ranch.

There was nothing else he could do.

Buxton was still tied up. The man was slumped over, leaning against his bonds. Spur searched the surrounding area. He saw the first tracks that he'd followed and his own right beside them.

Following them for a minute or two as they moved laterally from the ranch, Spur suddenly saw a second set turn to the left—into a clump of brush.

That must have been where he'd gone.

Hardwick had over an hour's lead on him, but unless the horse was supernaturally strong it would have to have a rest if Hardwick expected it to continue to transport him across the desert.

Spur crashed through the brush. New tracks, fresher tracks, led across a field of small dunes that had been kicked up by a wild wind.

Hardwick was clever. Too damn clever!

The image of Patti O'Brannigan's face rose before him. Spur quickly shook it out of his head as his horse trotted across the sand.

He never should have left St. Louis that day, Spur thought, peering at the real set of tracks. He should have taken a later train. He should have waited to see Fancy Freddie Hardwick's white neck broken by a stiff rope.

It wasn't his job—he'd done his part. And he had no idea that the murderer could escape. Still, he couldn't help but blame himself.

And that made him mad.

The outlaw squatted beneath a huge stone cliff that jutted from the ground. He sweated there, watched his mount and smiled.

McCoy had found him at the ranch. So what! He'd just hurried the inevitable. Hardwick realized that he should have killed the Secret

Service agent right then and there in the barn,
but where was the challenge in doing that?

No chase. No suspense. Just an explosion
and the sight of life oozing from his body.

And hell; he'd had enough of that for one day.
It had been a shame, though, he mused; Elijah
was pretty handy with a rifle and a revolver,
though he was a greenhorn. And the pretty
rancher's daughter might have been good for,
oh, a cold night or two. Or three.

"You up to another long, hard ride?"

The horse turned its head toward Hardwick.
As if comprehending the man's words, it
shuffled deeper into the shade. It's tail flicked
away a bothersome fly.

Hardwick thought of where he was heading.
It was the perfect place. McCoy wouldn't have
a chance. The fact that the man hadn't shown
yet indicated that the false trail he'd had Elijah
make that morning had worked.

Good, the outlaw thought.

Everything was going fine.

"Come on, girl," he said, rising with a grunt.
"We got some work to do!"

McCoy dipped into the hollows between the
dunes. The unusual landscape around him had
obviously contributed to their formation.
Wind, sliding down the craggy mounts to the
east, had scraped the desert floor. The low-
lying hills to the west had stopped the move-
ment of the sand and had thrown it onto itself.
Whenever it blew the sand dunes changed—
diminishing in one place, rising taller in
another.

Spur's mount protested as its hooves sank into the baking earth.

"Come on, boy," he said to the gelding. "It won't be long now."

A half-mile later, the horse whinneyed as it saw solid rock before it. They'd made it to the outskirts of the dunes, where the great sand sea abutted the shattered mountains. His mount's hooves clicked on the solid surface.

"That better for you?" he asked it, rubbing the horse's neck.

Spur's smile faded as he realized that Hardwick's tracks had vanished. A thin coating of sand blew back and forth over the sloping rock ledge.

Hardwick could be anywhere, McCoy thought. Knowing the bastard like he did, Spur knew it would be in the hardest place to find.

Far from him, a coyote howled at some disturbance.

Where should he start looking?

CHAPTER THIRTEEN

"Come on, McCoy," Hardwick said as he led his horse to the hundred-foot square, boxlike valley that pierced the rock. A spring bubbled up in its lower right-hand corner. Trees and shrubs choked the area around it.

Fred Hardwick smiled. He led his mount down the only passable trail that entered the box canyon. It had been smoothed out over the centuries by countless Indians. Sheer rock walls stuck straight up from the canyon floor all around him. He was glad he'd found it last week. It was perfect for his plan.

The box canyon looked as if it had been formed when God Himself had plucked out a square chunk of rock and sent it into the heavens.

The outlaw whistled an off-key tune. The horse cleared the last of the sand-strewn,

thirty-foot drop and trotted onto the earth. Its
nostrils flared at the smell of water. Hardwick
dismounted; the horse went directly to the
spring, lowered its head and drank.

Hardwick filled his canteen, tucked it inside
his shirt, removed his hat and returned to the
path that had deposited him within the box
canyon. As the sun burned into his white hair
and scalp, the man stooped and walked
backwards up the trail, brushing his hat over
the sand. Every so often he looked between his
legs to ensure that he wasn't also smoothing
over the horse tracks as he removed the signs
of his retreat from the box canyon.

The hat flicked back and forth in his hand.
Hardwick was sweating by the time he'd
reached the top.

The horse stood near the clump of trees and
bushes that soaked moisture from the spring.
They were thick enough to hide a human being.
Hardwick snickered and went to the place he'd
found earlier that day—the ledge from which
he had a clear view and a direct line of fire into
the canyon.

There was no sign of him. Spur had nearly
drained his canteen. This couldn't go on
forever, he told himself. He had to find the
man!

A patch of sand that had blown onto the rock
was empty of tracks. Cursing, McCoy rode on.
A mile later he came across another smooth
stretch of sand. Hoofprints stood out unmis-
takeably across its surface.

Hardwick!

Spur hurried his horse. He must be four

miles from the ranch by now. Hardwick was out there, somewhere, just waiting for him to ride up.

The rocky ridges undulated before him until they smashed up against the bulk of the bizarre mountains. It was wild, untamed country that didn't welcome his presence.

McCoy rubbed his mount's neck. He rode on, searching for more signs that Hardwick had come this way.

There were few. The rocky surface beneath him gave up no clues. An eerie wind occasionally howled past him, but no scent of smoke entered Spur's nostrils to betray a Hardwick-built fire. The ground was so uneven that he lacked a good view of the whole area.

He struggled up a particularly rough ridge. The angle was so steep that he soon dismounted and let his gelding scramble up it without his weight. Once he'd gained the top Spur moaned at the sight of yet more endless, spinelike projections of rock from the desert floor.

"Shit," he said.

His horse, however, sniffed the air. Its eyelids flashed past its huge brown eyes several times. Despite the heat and the rigors of their extended journey, it pranced forward.

"Hold on, boy!" Spur said.

Nothing stopped the horse. McCoy ran after it. His ankles soon ached at the incessant pounding of his boots on the solid rock. His mount slipped over a rise and disappeared. A distant horse whinneyed.

The sound of another horse's voice shocked Spur. Someone was there. Was it Hardwick?

He slowly trudged up the short, steep hill, silently pressing the soles of his boots against the rock.

The beast quieted but he thought he heard the sound of water bubbling nearby. Was it an illusion, he wondered? Could he possibly be hearing a mirage?

Wary of revealing his exact whereabouts, Spur skittered up the rise, removed his hat and peered over it.

It was no mirage. Bright green trees stood in the corner of a neat canyon. Sunlight shimmered on a pool of water and the stream that meandered from it sparkled like molten silver. His mount had aleady found a steep trail that led into the box canyon.

Spur tensed as he saw the strange horse standing at the spring. It answered the gelding's whinney and continued to slurp the sweet water.

Hardwick must be there. As sure as he might be that the false trail had fooled Spur, the man would never leave his horse in plain sight unless he'd planned a special reception for his pursuer.

Spur frowned and ducked back to safety behind the solid rock ridge.

He didn't have a rifle. He had only four extra rounds in his pocket, plus the six in his revolver. Hardwick could have an arsenal stashed in the trees, or somewhere above the canyon. He could even have compatriots.

Hardwick held all the cards, and he was itching to play his ace.

McCoy made a quick survey of the surrounding area. The spring must be the remnant of an ancient river that had carved the canyon out of solid rock. A millenia of falling water had shaped the hill around it into massive, smooth-edged ledges. There were literally dozens of holes and shadowy nooks large enough for a man to crawl into.

He plainly couldn't go into the canyon. That's what Hardwick would be wanting—a clear shot right through Spur's heart.

No.

He couldn't check the caves without putting himself into needless danger. Hardwick was out there.

Their horses stood side by side, drinking.

Both men without their mounts.

Spur wiped his forehead and put on his Stetson. It was hot. Boy, was it hot!

The water had drawn McCoy's horse right to it. Hardwick grinned as he slipped further into the blackness of his hole. The sinking sun behind him cast longer shadows across the canyon—across McCoy's death trap.

A human head flashed above the rock opposite him and quickly disappeared.

McCoy was there.

Hardwick scratched his chin after a few minutes. McCoy obviously smelled a trap. He hadn't followed his horse into the canyon. Perhaps that had been a bad idea, being so obvious. Maybe he'd underestimated the man.

The albino softly snorted as McCoy took another look around—too quick for him to get off a shot.

Damnit, he was being careful.

Fred Hardwick settled into his cubbyhole,

feeling the sun-heated rocks cradle his back. Wouldn't be good to challenge him, he thought, preparing to hold his position for as long as necessary. He'd outwait McCoy.

After all, he'd waited all this time since the man had had him condemned to death. What was another hour?

Spur was soon bored, clinging to the rocky ridge. The sun would set in two hours or less. At night he'd have an advantage over Hardwick—or, at least, more of one than he now had. If the outlaw didn't make a move, he wouldn't.

McCoy heard rustling in the canyon below him. Hooves against sand and rock. Just as he was about to peer into it again the man's horse pranced past him, sniffed the air, and trotted ten yards around the despression's perimeter. It tossed its head back and forth, as if searching for its master.

Come on, boy, Spur thought. Find him. Find Hardwick for me!

But the beautiful white animal soon seemed to lose interest in the search. The horse walked to the nearest shade and stood there contentedly.

Damn!

Grab hold of yourself, Hardwick!

The man shook his head. The rock walls seemed to be closing around him. Solid stone pressed hard against his spine, depressing the boney knobs that ran down it. Sweat soaked his clothing despite the relative coolness of the hole he'd chosen to hide in.

He glanced at his Spencer repeating rifle. He'd lain it beside his feet twenty minutes ago when he'd wearied of holding it. It would be there when he needed it.

His horse stood five yards away, resting under a tall ledge. McCoy hadn't shown his face again.

Fred wasn't used to this. He swept into a bank, took the money, killed everyone in sight, and swept out again. He'd had few endless standoffs like this and he didn't mind admitting that they weren't his glass of whiskey.

His back ached. Hardwick turned his head and twisted, trying to find a more comfortable position. His right cheek pressed against the overhead rock for a few seconds as he rearranged his feet.

That was better. The man wiped salty moisture from his upper lip.

Something brushed past his pant leg.

Hardwick froze. What the hell was it?

He reached for his rifle. His fingers closed around a warm, smooth surface that moved.

A sharp rattling echoed behind him. Trapped in a stooped position, unable to reach behind him, Hardwick looked outside. The shadowed rattlesnake shook its tail with increasing urgency.

Damn thing must have woken up on his rock, saw that the sun was setting and slithered in beside him. Just his luck, Hardwick thought.

Maybe McCoy wasn't watching. He gripped his rifle and burst from the hole as quietly as possible, moving toward the uncertain danger from the certain and real.

His mount flicked up its long head and ran

to him. He stepped into his saddle.

Spur heard a slight shuffling and the horse's hooves striking against the rock. Hardwick's horse must have grown bored. Would he reveal his owner's whereabouts?

He removed his hat and stuck his eyes just above the ridge. The white horse leapt over him, connected with the rock and slid down the hill.

Spur peeled off two shots before Hardwick was out of range. Neither of them hit the moving target. Cursing, he whistled to his own mount. The horse kept on drinking. McCoy turned back but Hardwick had already cleared the next ridge.

Those rental horses would be the death of him, he thought.

"Git yer butt up here!"

Spur ran down the path. He'd have to have a long talk with that horse—after he'd taken in Hardwick!

CHAPTER FOURTEEN

Not surprisingly, the outlaw hadn't bumped up and down over the ridges as he rode from the box canyon. Fred Hardwick's horse galloped between two of the rises. The bottom of the sand-filled depression was nearly level and provided both of their horses' good hoof-holds.

Spur's mount quickly fell into the spirit of the chase. He pushed the roan as hard as he could, urging her to run, to bring him within arm's reach of the notorious outlaw that rode far ahead.

"Come on, boy!" he said as the rocky ridges flashed past him on either side. "You'll have extra oats if you get me to that man!"

The deepening shadows made his mount unsure of its footing. It slowed as the sand grew thicker, even as Hardwick seemed to spurt faster away from him.

Frustrated, Spur nudged the horse closer to the rock wall. It balked at first, tossing its head, chomping at the bit. Soon, however, the solid ground beneath its shoes convinced it to obey his command.

He increased his speed.

Spur flew down the valley. The sound of his passage knocked back and forth between the rock walls. He started to gain on Hardwick again. It was an irritating game. Hardwick fell back, Spur sped up. The Secret Service agent's horse faltered on the slippery sand and the murderer slipped farther away from him.

"Come on!" he shouted.

Without a rifle, McCoy couldn't hope for an accurate shot at this distance. He closed the gap between the two charging horses. Closer. Closer!

Fred Hardwick suddenly vanished. The outlaw simply dropped out of sight. He hadn't turned off, he hadn't done anything. One second he'd been there. The next, the man and his mount were gone.

Spur pushed his horse harder, faster. His speed was so great that he couldn't rein it to a stop as the ground fell away below them.

Horse and rider tumbled twenty-feet straight down. The change of direction pitched McCoy from the saddle. He saw Hardwick scrambling up from the sand as he twisted through the air toward his inevitable meeting with the ground.

Spur took the impact. He was sore but everything felt fine. His horse pitifully whinneyed, lying on its side. One of its legs was bent backward at an unnatural angle. Hardwick's horse lay near it.

"Damn you!" Spur said as he rose and faced the enemy.

"Wait!" The albino raised his hands. "I'm unarmed! My rifle flew off somewhere and I can't find it!"

McCoy advanced on him. "You've got your face. That's weapon enough, Hardwick!"

"Don't shoot!" he said through his teeth. "This isn't fair!" His pink eyes were wild.

"You're already a dead man. You've added two more murders to your long string. Patti O'Brannigan and the kid you must have had working for you."

Hardwick's hat had flipped off. Spur was shocked to see the gleaming whiteness of his scalp. Most of the cream that he'd used to cover his face had dripped off from hours of sweating, revealing his true color.

"I never should have left you in St. Louis!" McCoy said. "It's too late for that. But if I took you in you'd just slip your ass out of jail again. That isn't going to happen, Hardwick. I'm gonna carry out Judge Stone's sentence right here." Spur cocked his revolver.

The albino grinned. "Hell, McCoy! You're a man of the law. You'd never do something as illegal as that! Why, it'd torture you for years if you—"

"Shut your fucking mouth, Hardwick!"

The downed horses behind him filled the air with agonized sounds.

The outlaw narrowed his eyebrows. "Look, McCoy, ah, maybe we can work something out. I've done a couple of jobs, have some money stashed away."

"I told you to cork your trap!"

"Shit, McCoy! There isn't a government man anywhere that can't be bought."

He walked to the man and stopped four feet away.

The slanting sun made Hardwick's face glow like a snowball with pink eyes. A coyote howled in the distance. Spur's trigger finger ached.

"Hey!" the outlaw said, raising his hands. "What's a few murders and a few thousand dollars between friends?" He snarled and rushed McCoy.

Spur fired. The bullet found its mark deep within Fred Hardwick's chest. It lodged in the surprised man's heart. The murderer stared at McCoy in shock. His body reeled. Hardwick took a tentative step forward. He slammed a hand over the small hole in his shirt and fell.

McCoy pumped another bullet into the man, then fired a third shot, the last for Patti O'Brannigan, the beautiful, sweet rancher's daughter who'd never hurt anyone and would never live the life she'd barely started.

Hardwick's body shook as the red-hot lead pierced it. The explosions which accompanied Spur's marksmanship drifted away on the wind, carrying with them a bluish smoke and the life of the notorious outlaw.

Spur wiped his upper lip. He looked at what was left of Fred Hardwick and went to the horses. His mount's foreleg was broken. There was nothing he could do. He mercifully dispatched it with one shot. McCoy turned to Hardwick's mount. It lay as if dead. Spur's boot touched its broad back.

To his surprise it folded its legs and sprang

up, fit and fully functional. His shock was soothed with relief.

"You were faking, eh?" He rubbed the beast's neck. "Hardwick sure trained you well. What should we do with the ugly old bastard, huh?"

No sense in taking him back to town. The man was already dead. Besides, McCoy couldn't stomach the trip with him. He'd leave him here.

Ten minutes later, Spur had kicked away enough sand with his boots to dig a shallow grave. He unceremoniously dumped Hardwick's body into the hole and covered it over. Using his pocket knife, he tore a flap from one of Hardwick's saddlebags and, with its tip, engraved some words onto its smooth, stained surface:

> *"Fast Freddy Hardwick*
> *lies here*
> *None too soon"*

It was over. He'd never know how long the man had been robbing banks, or how many of the thefts that he'd been sent to investigate had been his work. Spur was fairly certain that Buxton had done some of them.

Buxton. The man should still be tied up back at the O'Brannigan ranch.

Spur stared down at the lifeless bulk of his horse. At leaast it looked like it was at peace.

"Sorry what I said about you back there." Spur's voice was soft. He cleaned out his old mount's bags, transferred the few supplies to his new horse, stepped into the saddle and rode away, back toward the ranch and, he hoped, a still bound Burt Buxton.

It was well after dusk by the time McCoy dragged into the O'Brannigan ranch. He tied up next to a magnificent black stallion who had only recently returned home, judging from its recent brushing.

He went directly to the porch where he'd tied up the man. Buxton wasn't there. Light coming from the house put him on the defensive again. He quickly reloaded, went up the three stairs and walked inside.

"Come any closer and you'll be singing hymns in hell!" a grizzled, white-haired man screamed as he stared down the barrels of his shotgun.

It must be Patti O'Brannigan's rancher father. "I'm Spur McCoy, a lawman."

"Yup. I'll just bet ye are!" His gaze burned into Spur's. "What are ye doing back here, want to finish the job? Kill all of us?"

"Mr. O'Brannigan?" McCoy asked. The man's wrinkled cheeks were wet.

"You know damn well!"

"I'm—"

"Just got home an hour ago. I thought she'd still be in town, but I went upstairs and I—I found her—" The rifle shook in his hands.

"The man responsible for that is dead. I just killed him out by the box canyon."

Edgar O'Brannigan's head fell.

"There were three of them when I got here," Spur said, casually holstering his revolver. "There was nothing I could do to stop them."

"But she was—she was just a little girl," the man blubbered.

"Please, O'Brannigan, where's the man I had tied to your front porch?"

Edgar's work-hewn body shook. "My Patti. She was the best thing that ever happened to me, the only thing I had left save for this ranch after my missus died."

"Mr. O'Brannigan!" Spur shouted. "I know this is a bad time, but—"

"What?" he violently asked.

"You heard my question," McCoy said gently.

"I know. Hell, lawman, I—I—"

"Please!"

"I let him go."

The words burned into McCoy's brain. "You what?"

The rancher looked up at Spur. "And what the hell wuz I supposed to do? Tell me that! He said he'd escorted Patti out here from town and some bandits attacked them just as they were getting out of the buggy."

"Not true!"

O'Brannigan dropped into a rail-backed chair. "Them bandits tied them both up out there, then they changed their minds and took her upstairs. That feller told me he was knocked on the head and beat up. From the looks of him, I believed him. He said he didn't know what happened after that . . . ." The rancher's voice trailed off.

"It's a lie, O'Brannigan. He was one of them! I was the one who tied him up!"

The rancher dropped his rifle onto his knees

and hugged himself. The middleaged man shivered.

"I understand your grief," Spur said. "But like I said, the man who killed your daughter has been punished. I'll be leaving you now."

"What was his name?" McCoy went towards the door.

"What? Ah, who?"

"The man who killed my daughter!"

"Fred Hardwick."

O'Brannigan spat. "That's what I think of him. May he burn in hell forever!"

"Amen," Spur said. He slipped from the ranchhouse.

Where would a two-bit bank robber go in the middle of the desert? Where would Buxton hide himself?

There was only one place he would go. Back to Deadridge.

Spur hoped Hardwick's horse was up to another long, hard ride.

CHAPTER FIFTEEN

Judging from the position of the moon in the darkened sky it must be nearly ten, Spur thought as he rode into Deadridge. Hardwick's horse was a sure-footed, sprightly beast, and had obeyed McCoy's commands without hesitation. The well-trained mount seemed to be able to see in the darkness and had rarely misplaced a hoof.

Spur had ridden directly to Deadridge and the Deluxe Hotel from O'Brannigan's ranch. He gave his mount a quick rub down and went to Kitty Carson's room. He smiled at her, ah, unusual name. Where'd she ever pick it up?

McCoy softly knocked on her hotel room's door. There was no answer.

"Kitty?" Spur yelled, rapping with more force on the plain rectangle of wood. Again, he heard nothing.

Was she in danger? Had Buxton come back to avenge himself, or had he already carried her off?

"Kitty, open the door. It's Spur McCoy!"

A faint rustle from inside the room convinced him. It soon silenced. Spur tried the knob. It wouldn't move. He drew and powered his boot against the door.

It popped open. Spur ran inside.

The light was blinding. Three kerosene lamps illuminated the scene. The curtains were closed. Kitty Carson smiled as she rose from the bed, adjusting her dress. Burt Buxton cleared his throat, hesitated and stood. The fully dressed man glared at him and slapped his thigh. Spur had obviously interrupted something.

"What the hell kind of man are you, barging into a woman's private hotel room?" he demanded.

"Keep your pants on, Buxton. The game's over."

"What game?" he asked.

"I know you tried to break into the Deadridge Bank. Kitty told me. If old man O'Brannigan hadn't let you go you'd be behind bars by now!"

"What?" The young woman fastened a few of the buttons that ran up the front of her bodice and crossed her legs. She flicked brown hair from her eyes.

Buxton pointed toward Kitty. "Hell! She must've told you some kind of story. And you believed it?" He shook his head. "The wench was just sore at me, that's all."

"You put up a pretty good fight back at the ranch," Spur pointed out.

Buxton coughed. "Sir, I was just defending myself against your vicious and sudden attack."

"Sure. What were you doing out there with one of the most notorious and reviled murderers and bank thiefs that's ever worked the west? Gossiping, I suppose? Maybe exchanging flapjack recipes?"

Kitty straightened her back. "Fred Hardwick? Oh, Burt, you didn't! That disgusting white freak! I'd heard he might be in town but—" She clasped a hand over her mouth.

Buxton glanced around the room. Spur followed his gaze until it stopped at the man's holster lying on the floor near McCoy's boots. Buxton must have hung it over the doorknob and it had fallen during the Secret Service agent's sudden entrance into the room.

Spur smirked. "Your game is up, Buxton. You're coming with me."

"Where to?" he sneered as he sat beside Kitty on the bed. "There's no jail in this town. No place to put me. Besides, I didn't do anything. You know you can't prove it. Back out of her nice-like and let me get to what I was just about to do to Miss Carson."

Something wasn't right, Spur thought. Kitty had said she detested the man, and yet here she was, with him of her own free will. There were no signs that he had forced her into doing anything. Most curious.

McCoy lowered his aim. "Stand up now, Buxton. Or you'll lose a ball."

"Spur, really!" Kitty said.

"Whatever you say. I never argue with a man who's holding a firearm. But you don't have any proof!" He rose. "I'll never be convicted. Besides, the bank wasn't robbed."

"Attempted robbery," McCoy said.

Buxton frowned. "And no one was killed."

"Fred Hardwick took care of that. He killed two people out at the ranch. One of them was a woman."

"That wasn't me! I got thrown off the train when the conductor found out I didn't have a ticket. I just stopped there to get a drink of water! That desert's hot!"

"Sure, sure," Spur said. He kicked the man's gunbelt behind him.

Kitty started to speak, bit her lip and smiled.

"I didn't try to rob the bank," Buxton said. "But why don't you ask her what she was doing last night?" he nodded toward his female companion.

"What are you saying?" Kitty asked.

He leered. "Ask her how I met her."

The woman laughed. "Come on, Burt! Don't try to be clever. You're not smart enough."

"Tell me your story, Buxton."

"Really, Spur, its—"

"Shut up, Kitty! Let the man talk!"

The thief tucked in his plaid shirt. "Well, I was walking down the alley behind the bank. I saw the back door open, thought that was rather curious, and so I went in." He glanced at Kitty Carson. "I saw missy here bending over beside the safe—and she looked good enough to eat. The whole place stunk of her nose-twisting perfume. I surprised her; she screamed, some guy with a rifle woke up and took a shot at us. We ran. That's all I know."

Kitty Carson smoothed her skirt over her knees. "I've heard better stories from folks who couldn't talk!"

"Is this true, Kitty?" Spur advanced on her, still aiming between Buxton's legs.

She narrowed her eyebrows. "Of course not! I'm just a woman, after all."

"Who just happens to be named after a renowned scout? I don't think so. A woman changes her name when she's hiding something—just like a man."

Kitty arched her eyebrows. "Really, Spur?"

It all made sense. Kitty was in the bank that night. But he didn't believe all of Buxton's story. Had they run into each other accidentally in some other way?

"Okay, Buxton. Let's say what you're telling me is true. Then why'd you come back here?"

"Well, ah, me and the woman had some unfinished business to attend to."

"Uh-huh. Go on."

Buxton wiped his forehead. "Where should I have gone? There isn't another town around here for a hundred miles. And no train or stage coming through. So I came back here to visit with Miss Carson."

"Sure." Spur smiled.

"It's the truth!"

"No it isn't!" Kitty stood. "I told you the truth when I saw you as the train left early this morning! He tried to crack the safe in the Deadridge Bank!"

"And I suppose he was wearing your perfume while he was doing it?"

Kitty folded her hands. "Obviously you're beyond normal reasoning."

"I don't know just what went on in the bank that night, except that there were two people in men's clothing. Let's see . . . ."

McCoy walked to the free-standing walnut closet and flipped open its mirrored door. A dusty pair of trousers and a plain cotton shirt popped out, followed by one man's boot. It was dusty and quite small.

"Dressing up for the cotillion, Miss Carson?" Spur smirked at her.

"Those—those are his things!" Kitty said.

He kicked up the shirt, grabbed it and smelled its collar. "Buxton, you have fine taste in perfume!"

"Now see here!" he yelled, looking once again at his fallen gunbelt. "I'm outraged at your implication!"

"You were obviously both there. You wanna tell me about it—or wait to tell the judge?"

Gazes flashed between them. Spur felt the room tense. Kitty finally sighed.

"Okay!" Kitty said. "I give up. You tell him, Burt." She fanned herself.

"Well . . . ."

"Look. We can't do anything about it. Let's just tell him, you big ape! I'll go first."

"Heck, Kitty!"

"Shut up, Buxton!"

The man sat beside the woman.

Kitty Carson looked at the ceiling. "I started robbing some stores about two months ago. It was an easy way to make money, lots easier than working in a saloon. Then I tried my first bank. I caught the manager putting some money into the safe, convinced him to give it all to me and took the morning stage out of town."

"Where was that?" Spur asked.

Kitty rubbed her chin. "I think that was in Lobo, but I can't be sure. After that I guess I just got lucky. I must have hit, oh, three or four banks. At least."

Buxton groaned. "With your technique? Hell, Kitty; you darn near tripped over the guard the other night!"

She turned to him. "That's becuase I ran into you! I couldn't believe you were trying to break into the same bank at the same time!"

That was it. McCoy smiled. Everything fell into place. There had been three of them—Hardwick, Kitty and Buxton. Three thieves, all robbing banks in the general area. None had ever met until the last two days.

"Go on, Miss Carson," Spur said.

Kitty bent and scratched her ankle inside her boot. "That's all there is to tell about me. But Burt told me all about his work in the last few months. He must have hit six or seven banks in small towns all over the area—Arizona and California. He said he's got money stashed along trails from the village of San Diego right across to Tucson!"

"You have some kind of record of where you stashed all this money?" Spur asked.

"Yeah." He tapped his head. "Up here where you'll never find it, asshole!" He turned to Kitty. "Did anyone ever tell you you talk too much?" Buxton said.

"Yes." She suddenly turned and kissed his mouth.

Buxton didn't resist. Their hands met. Burt returned the kiss with surprising passion. They grappled on the bed. Kitty's skirts went flying.

"If we could—Kitty, Buxton!" Spur said.

The man removed his lips from the young woman's mouth and raised his eyebrows. "Be with you in a second, McCoy!"

"No. Now!" he shouted.

Ignoring him, Buxton kissed her again. Spur went to them and shook the outlaw's shoulder. Kitty tried to push him away.

"Can't you see we're, ah, having a moment of tender passion? Butt out, Spur!"

"You're both under arrest!"

They broke their kiss. Buxton gave him a tight-lipped smile.

He moved fast.

Cold steel kissed Spur's flesh. The knife slid into his right arm.

Pain stabbed through him. McCoy's Colt nearly tumbled from his fingers.

CHAPTER SIXTEEN

Spur jerked back from the deadly slice of the knife in his right arm. He cursed and smashed the butt of his Colt .44 onto Buxton's head, sending the man spiraling to the bed.

Kitty Carson jumped onto McCoy's back, kicking and scratching and all arms and legs. Spur easily stood; the young woman fell onto her fellow bank thief.

The wound wasn't bad, McCoy thought as he looked it over. Just a little nick. But he was sure the man had been aiming for his hand.

"I've had it with you, Buxton!" Spur yelled. "Give me one good reason not to kill you!"

The man rubbed his forehead. He closed his eyes and pushed Kitty off of his torso.

"You slipped him a knife, eh?" Spur said as Kitty turned flashing emerald eyes toward him. "My, you are smooth, girl. But not smooth enough."

She shrugged and smiled. "There isn't a jail here in Deadridge," she said. "My, Mr. McCoy, what *are* you going to do with us?"

Spur smiled. "I can find a place to dump the two of you until I can escort you to the Territorial prison in Yuma. Don't worry yourself about that, Kitty!"

She sighed and finally noticed that the buttons that had held up her dress had popped off, revealing her creamy chemise. "Getting a good eyeful, Spur?" she said, noticing that his gaze had temporarily dropped.

"Don't count on it." He heard male voices behind him. Must be out in the hall. "The excitement's over, folks," McCoy said without turning around. "Go about your business!"

Kitty turned to the opened door. "No. Ah, boys, come on in! Free show right now!"

"Alright!"

Six men pushed past Spur. His shouts did nothing to quench their excitement. Kitty stood and gyrated her hips, running slender fingers up and down her thighs.

"This what you boys came to see?" she asked as she licked her lips. "Compliments of the Deluxe Hotel. Everyone crowd around to see Kitty's Erotic Dances of Egypt!"

"Gentlemen. Gentlemen!" McCoy shouted.

It was no use. The six men shoved around Spur, ignoring him. Kitty smiled through the sea of human heads. Buxton managed to pull himself partially from the bed. He groaned and crashed to the floor, rubbing his head.

The spectators hooted at Kitty's shameless

display. The noise grew louder as she ripped off her chemise, exposing her prefectly round, pink-tipped breasts.

"Goddamn!" one man said.

"Yeah, girlie! Show us the rest of yer stuff!"

"This is better than New Orleans!"

Spur bellowed at the men but, understandably, they weren't listening to him. They were spellbound by the sight of Kitty Carson's flesh, pretty female flesh.

McCoy fired a shot into the ceiling, wincing as the new knife-wound in his arm burned. Maybe it had done some damage, he thought.

The woman stopped. The men turned toward him.

"What the hell you doing, stopping the show?" a mean-faced man asked him.

"I'm a lawman. This man and woman are my prisoners. They tried to rob the Deadridge Bank."

"That cute thang?" a blue-eyed youth said. "You've been drinking!"

A red-haired, grizzled man laughed. "Heck. He just wants to keep her for himself."

"Yeah! Move on, stranger, and let the girl dance her heart out!"

"And her clothes off!"

Spur blasted another shot into the ceiling. Wood splintered. The explosion vibrated within Kitty's hotel room.

"Out. All of you. Now!"

The assembled men grumbled, glanced at each other and filed from the room. As the last man left, Spur slammed the door and hefted Buxton's gunbelt. "Now, you two, do what I say. Or there'll never be another show!"

Buxton's head fell to his chest. Kitty dressed. Spur found a pink silk scarf in the woman's wardrobe.

"This should do just nicely," he said.

"For what?" The woman struggled into a clean chemise and did up the buttons on the bodice of her dress.

"Turn around. I'll show you."

Buxton seemed to be unconscious. Spur tightly bound together the woman's hands with the silk scarf. Blood oozed from his wounded arm.

"Hey!" she said, struggling against the knot.

"Just temporary, but at least it's silk. I got a feeling I can't trust you."

"Really, Spur!" Kitty said as she turned to face him. "After all we've meant to each other?"

"Cute," he smirked. "Your friend Buxton seems to be taking a nap."

"I'm not surprised, the way you beat him up!" Kitty said, slicing her words.

"Sit down. On the bed!"

She met his gaze. "Make me!"

A quick push accomplished that. Spur checked Buxton's pulse and then his eyes. He was alilve but unconscious. McCoy ripped a cord from the curtains and bound the man to one leg of the brass bed. "That should keep him for a bit while we take a walk," he said to the beautiful woman.

Kitty tossed her head. "What makes you think I'm going anywhere with you?"

"Come on." He motioned with his revolver. "Be a good little whore, bank thief, and whatever the hell else you are!"

The woman pushed up from the bed, still bound. "Where are we going? All the way to Yuma?"

"No. To the bank."

"The bank?" Kitty laughed. "You going to let me empty the safe after all? And I thought you didn't like me anymore!"

"I don't. But I have a feeling there's someone at the bank who's going to be very pleased to see you and your partner."

"Burt Buxton is not my partner!" she said.

"Move it, angel-face!"

Spur opened the door and pushed Kitty outside. They attracted some stares as they went through the lobby and outside. The Deadridge Bank was a block away, and Spur had soon prodded the woman to it.

McCoy banged on the front door. Curly Ames greeted him with a shotgun.

"McCoy!" the banker said. "What's this?"

"One of the 'men' who broke into your bank the other night."

"A woman?" The beefy man snorted and shook his head. "Well I'll be! You were right!"

"Keep an eye on her. She's as slippery as an eel. Just put her in a chair and don't, I repeat, don't let her do or say anything." He looked at the woman. "If she tries to get away shoot her. Just shoot her."

Ames nodded. "Sure thing, McCoy."

"I'll be right back with her partner."

"He's *not* my partner!" Kitty said.

Spur returned to the woman's hotel room. The man was still unconscious, so he dragged him to the bank, threw Buxton over his shoulder and carried him in.

"That the other one?" Ames said.

McCoy nodded and placed him in a chair opposite an unusually sedate Kitty Carson. "Yep. Between the two of them—if I can believe what the lady told me—they've pulled well over ten bank robberies in the last few months."

"I'll be!" Ames whistled. "And she's such a pretty thing, too!"

"Don't let her fool you. She's got the body of Venus and the—"

"Don't get poetic on me!" Kitty said.

He groaned. "Ames, when's the next stage or train out of town? Toward Yuma?"

The banker rubbed his chin. "Noon stage tomorrow, but it's heading in the other direction. No, that's right, that was the last schedule. It does go to Yuma."

"Then we'll be on it. Do you think you could keep an eye on these two tonight?"

Ames smiled and gripped his shotgun with both hands. "I think me and my friend could be talked into it."

"Good. See you in the morning."

"Right, McCoy. Thanks."

"Spur!" the woman called.

He kept walking toward the door.

"Spur McCoy, you turn around and look at me!"

It was difficult to ignore Kitty's voice.

"Alright, then. Don't look at me. Just please stop and listen!"

Spur halted and faced the woman. Kitty slumped in her chair. Her face was solemn.

"I'll listen to you."

She brightened.

"All the way to Yuma. Try to get some sleep, Kitty. You'll need it!"

He walked out to the tune of Ames' laughter.

Spur moved the kerosene lamp where it wouldn't cast their shadows on his room's windowshade. That finished, he checked the lock on the door and sat to remove his boots.

"I sure was surprised to see you," he said as he tugged the stiff leather past his toes.

The woman behind him on the bed laughed.

"I figured you'd be hell and highwater from Deadridge by now. I guess you changed your plans."

She meowed.

His second boot hit the floor. Spur stood and quickly undressed. "Just couldn't stay away from me, could you? Yeah. I have that effect on women. All women."

A laugh.

"Well, some women." He pulled off his shirt. "Maybe you just couldn't leave without saying goodbye. Don't we have some unfinished business?"

Silence.

"I'm bruised, banged up, bleeding and bone-tired." He dropped his trousers. "I should have a bath," McCoy said. "Shouldn't I?"

Annemarie smiled at him from the bed. "You talk too much, Spur McCoy. Come here."

"No promises," he said. "I hope I don't disappoint you, after that night we spent on the train."

She flicked her tongue between her lips and shook her bare bottom. "I'm not worried."

Spur thrust down his long underwear. He

turned to the beautiful woman. "Annemarie, what am I going to do with you?"

She was on her stomach on the bed, facing him, watching his every move. Brilliant tresses of blond hair billowed around her face. Her blue eyes shone.

"You know exactly what you're going to do with me, Spur McCoy!"

He'd been surprised to see her in the lobby of the Deluxe Hotel. Not waiting for an explanation, he'd taken Annemarie's arm and led the woman to his hotel room. She hadn't spoken a word until just now.

"Yeah, I suppose I do, Annemarie."

She flipped the Stetson from his head. "I'm not expecting a miracle man," the woman softly said. "You've been out doing whatever it is you do. You're weary and aching all over." She shook her head. "Let's see what we can do about that. After all, even if it isn't as good as the first time—and sometimes it isn't—it'll be better than sleeping alone."

He kissed her left breast, sucking the warm flesh, feeling it harden between his lips. "I'll eat to that."

CHAPTER SEVENTEEN

Spur sighed at the liquid sensation that poured through him. Standing, he looked down at the top of Annemarie's bobbing blonde head. Hands clutched his muscled buttocks. Their flesh slid together.

McCoy groaned and gently pumped.

She pulled away from him and flashed a smile. "Do you like this?" she asked. "Or are you just putting up with it because I like doing it to you?"

"I hate it," Spur said. "It's pure torture."

She nipped the head of his erection.

"Hey!" Spur said.

Her laugh was muffled. Annemarie pulled him harder into her. Spur's naked body trembled as he went deeper into her yielding throat.

"Mmmmmmm!"

"Don't talk with your mouth full!" he said.

His testicles brushed her chin time and time again. The woman was amazing.

"Oh God!"

Spur had never met a woman who could take the whole thing, yet here she was, demanding more, almost furiously forcing him to pump his penis in and out of her throat.

His body tightened. McCoy felt his knees go weak. He firmly pried the woman's fingers from his buttocks and stepped back.

Annemarie stared up at him. Her lips glistened. She licked them.

"What's wrong, honey?" she asked, taking his erection in her hand. She squeezed it.

"Let's slow down." Spur moaned at the erotic contact. He backed out of her reach.

"Spur!"

"Now now, Annemarie. All things in good time."

She watched him throb before her and grinned. "All things come to those who wait?"

"Yeah. And it almost did—come, I mean. How the hell can you do that so well?"

"Do what?"

"You know what I mean!"

The blue eyed beauty slipped her left hand between her legs. "I was excited. You excited me. When I'm that way I lose all shame. He's a challenge. I rose to it, I guess."

"Let me look at you again." McCoy lifted the woman. Annemarie posed for him.

She was so comfortable in her nudity. No delicate flower, this was all woman. Her breasts weren't too large, weren't too small. Her torso narrowed at her waist. Flaring, rounded hips melted into her beautiful legs.

Her nipples were stiff and wet from when he'd soaked them with his saliva. The patch of blonde fur between her legs rose out, inviting him to visit.

"Turn around," he said with a grin.

"Yes sir."

Annemarie faced the wall. Spur sighed at the beauty of her white shoulders, the curve of her back and the swell of her full bottom.

"Do I please you?" she asked.

"You know you do." Spur spun her to face him. His erection touched her belly. They both looked down and laughed.

"We have to do something about that," the woman said. "And I know just what to do."

"In a minute."

He picked her up and placed her on the bed. McCoy lifted Annemarie's legs, knelt and pushed his mouth onto her fur. She smelled so good! He found what he was looking for, licked and teethed it.

"Uhhh."

Spur spread apart her legs and went to work, sucking her clitoris. Annemarie thrashed on the bed as his tongue flicked over her hardened button.

"That's not fair!" she said.

Spur ate harder.

"Not—not fair—"

The taste of her musk stimulated him. He savagely forced her to the ultimate experience, sucking and eating until Annemarie cried out, pushing her undulating body harder against his face, gasping and panting as pure sensation shot through her.

The woman ground her opening to his mouth. Spur prolonged her orgasm, stretching it until she squirmed and grasped his head.

"Stop!" she said.

"Okay. I'll stop that."

He dropped onto her soft form. They shared a genital-flavored kiss.

"It's time you did it," Annemarie said.

"The lady's always right."

She slapped her palms to his chest, trying to push him off her.

"Hey! I thought you said you wanted to do it!"

"Yes, but not the missionary way."

"Oh." He moved to the bed.

Annemarie leered at him and got on all fours. She stuck her bottom out at him. "Come at me from behind, Spur! Do it from behind!"

He rubbed his hands together and stood. Everything lined up just fine. "You want it hard and fast, Annemarie, or slow and deep?"

"Yes!" She impatiently bumped herself against his erection. "Hurry before I go mad!"

Spur gripped the base of his erection and rubbed it against the woman's lips. Her wet heat was too pleasant for him to put it off any longer.

Annemarie trembled as their bodies connected. He pushed into her with one thrust, driving deeper and deeper. The woman gasped and writhed.

"Spur, is that all of it?" she asked hopefully as he stopped.

"Almost."

He slid in the last inch.

Annemarie sighed as he touched parts of her

that had never been touched by any man. The fit was perfect, as if it were tailor-made.

"You ought to be arrested. You're so big!"

"That's what I was born with." He bent over her and took her hanging breasts, squeezing Annemarie's nipples between his fingers.

"You—you were born with that—that huge thing?"

He chuckled. "Okay. So it grew."

"I'll—I'll say!"

Spur McCoy reared back and pushed into her. He released her breasts, straightened up and gripped the woman's waist. Her pleasure fueled his own. He pumped, flexing his buttocks, sliding into her with long, deep thrusts. Blonde hair flew around her head. His thighs slapped her upturned cheeks.

"Heaven," she sighed. "This is heaven."

"Yeah, woman. I feel so spiritual, putting it into your lovely slot."

"I told you Spur; sometimes you talk too much!"

"Oh, I'm sorry, ma'am. I thought you might want to hear how much I've been wanting this, how much I've wanted to fuck you again since that night on the train. But if you don't want me to tell you about it, I'll shut up."

Their bodies banged together at the middle. Sweat sprung out on McCoy's brow.

"Do you like it?" he asked, accentuating the question with a harder push.

"You know I do! Give me your thing!"

She pushed backward, meeting him halfway, forcing him faster into her. They were crazed, lusty animals. Spur rode her so hard that she trembled through two almost simultaneous orgasms.

"Grab my hair!"

"What?" he asked as he worked behind her.

"I said, grab my hair!"

He took a handful of blonde hair and gently tugged on it.

"Yeah. Now—now do it as quick as you can!"

Spur obliged. He rode her like a horse. Annemarie arched her back. Her head flew up and down as he pushed into her. His control started to fade. His body tightened. Annemarie squeezed around him as she shuddered through yet another climax.

That did it. Spur let go of her hair and grabbed her waist. He grunted and thrust violently into her. The woman sobbed in pure pleasure. The brass bed shook so violently that the mattresses almost fell off.

McCoy closed his eyes. He pumped his seed into her, draining his testicles, shivering and groaning at the overwhelming release. The woman slammed her hips backward. His thrusts were spastic. Uncontrolled. Totally satisfying.

It seemed to go on and on. Spur felt one last bit spurt from his penis. He shook so violently that he collapsed onto her back. His lips found her neck. Annemarie flattened on the bed. He slipped out of her.

A breeze cooled Spur's wet back. He licked the woman's neck as he fought to regain control of his senses. Annemarie turned her head and they kissed.

It was a tender, erotic embrace of lips and tongue. McCoy took her head in his hands and tasted her mouth. She moaned and sucked.

They parted a minute later. Spur rolled off her back and plopped onto the mattress beside her. Annemarie put her hands under her chin and smiled at him.

"You know something?" she asked, flushed with the vigorous exercise they'd just enjoyed.

"What's that?"

"It was better than on the train. Much better."

Spur grinned. "Thanks. But it does take two."

"Two?" Annemarie licked her lips. "I'd say you have at least ten down there."

"The way you talk!"

She pressed her right cheek to his hairy chest. "I'm listening to your heart," the woman said.

"Really?" He stroked her yellow hair. "What's it saying to you?"

"It's saying . . ." She paused. "Tick . . . tick . . . tick . . . Spur has a big dick."

He laughed. "You're such a poet, my dear! Wordsworth trapped in a woman's body."

"Mmm. I like this body."

"So do I, Annemarie. So do I."

"What were you doing out there? I mean, that you got stabbed and everything? Between the times that we—did it?"

He sighed. "Oh, the usual. Nearly getting hanged. Beating up other men. Falling off cliffs. Shooting at horse-mounted thieves."

She trailed her hand down his chest to his stomach. "Really?"

"Yeah. Riding across the burning desert with almost no water. Jumping out of windows. Getting—"

"How exciting." She gripped him.

"Exciting?"

"Yes." Annemarie lifted her eyebrows. "That's what I like about men."

"What. That?" He pushed up his hips.

"No. The fact that they're always doing something . . . exciting."

He grinned. "Annemarie, I—wait! I just realized that I don't even know your last name!"

"You never asked me." She insiduously worked on his limp penis.

"What is it?"

"Carson," she said. "Annemarie Carson."

He lifted his head. "You're not related to Kitty Carson, are you?"

"Who?"

"Ah, never mind. Just keep doing what you're doing."

He fell back and kissed the top of her head, full of the satisfying feeling of having finished two assignments.

CHAPTER EIGHTEEN

"Talk!"

The man turned his head away from Spur as he sat bound to a chair in Curly Ames' bank. "Not until hell freezes over!" Burt Buxton said.

McCoy leaned over him. Early morning sunlight splashed through the bank's windows. "Tell me where you hid the money that you stole during your bank robberies."

"Not on your life."

"How about on yours?" Spur patted his holster.

Buxton stared at him. "You wouldn't dare! I've never killed anyone! All I did was rob banks!"

Spur's fingers closed around the butt of his pistol. "Is that all you have to say to me?" He scowled. "I don't give a damn about you, Buxton. You're dirt. No one would notice if I rubbed out your worthless life."

He strained against his bonds. "Yeah sure. But if you plug me you'll never find the money. You need me, McCoy. You need me and you know it!"

Spur let his revolver rest in his holster. "Most assholes like you keep a map of some kind showing where they buried the money. Did you, Buxton?"

He quickly glanced at his front pants pocket. "No way! I'm not that stupid."

Spur grinned and bent over. He forced a hand into the stiff cloth compartment.

"Not on the first date," Buxton said.

Spur shoved deeper. The man's pocket was stretched tight against his thigh. Spur finally felt the edge of a piece of folded paper inside it.

"Stand up!" he barked.

Buxton shook his head. "I'm tied to this god-damned chair! How am I supposed to stand up?"

"Do it!"

He sighed and shifted his weight forward. "Rock back and forth."

Buxton's chair finally tilted. He lifted its back two legs from the floor.

"Very good. Maybe after you're released from jail you can get a job as a trained bear."

"Shut up!" Burt hissed.

The new position allowed Spur to reach into the man's pocket. He retrieved the paper and pushed Buxton's chair back to the marble-tiled floor.

"What have we here?" he said. It had been folded many times. Spur spread it out on the desk and studied it. "I thought so. Buxton, you aren't smart enough to put on your boots. This map's so easy to decipher it's pitiful!"

"Hah!"

"The big star in the middle's Yuma. To the right is Tucson, and the circle marks the coast of California. I'll find the money you stole, Buxton, while you're rotting in jail."

"Like hell I will!"

Spur stood before him again and pocketed the map. Burt Buxton sneered at him.

"If they lock me up I'll wait. I'll find a way to get out of jail and I'll hunt you down like a rabbit. Know what I'll do when I find you, McCoy?"

"Kiss me hello?"

Buxton rattled the chair's legs on the floor, violently straining against the thick ropes.

"Save it for later," Spur said. "You'll need your strength. It's a long trip to Yuma."

Buxton hung his head.

McCoy had arranged to question the two suspects alone. Curly Ames brought in Kitty and rustled out Buxton. The woman was sleepy eyed as she sat before him.

"Kitty, do you realize the seriousness of the charges that will be brought before you?"

"Yes. I'm no idiot, Mr. McCoy."

"You must be to have done what you did. How did a woman like you ever get involved in thievery?"

She sighed. "I told you. It was the easiest way to make money."

He knelt in front of her. "Maybe the judge'll

go easy on you. After all, you did help me find
Buxton."

"And that murdering Fancy Freddie!" She
shivered and closed her emerald eyes. "If I'd
known that Burt was the kind of man who'd
associate with killers like that I never would
have spoken to him."

"Hmmmm. Kitty, where were the banks you
robbed? What towns were they?"

She whistled.

"Answer my question, Kitty!"

The woman broke into an old hymn.

Spur laughed and covered her mouth with
his hand. "Tell me one thing, would you? I'm
curious. What's your real name? It certainly
isn't Kitty Carson."

"Mmmphsgle," she said.

Spur peeled off his hand. The woman pursed
her lips.

"It's Grace Kenyon."

"Why would you want to change it? And why
Kitty Carson?"

She tossed her head. "I met this woman on
the train. Annemarie Carson was her name. I
liked her last name so much that I decided to
use it in this town."

"I see. And what about Kitty?"

"I made that up." She smiled. "It just seemed
to go with it. I don't know."

Spur nodded. "I'll get the information I need
from you one way or the other. If you cooper-
ate I'll try to persuade the judge to reduce your
sentence."

"I'm not going to jail," she said, training her
flashing eyes on his. "I couldn't survive in
there."

"Then tell me what I want to know, woman! Which banks did you rob?"

She pressed her lips together and smiled. "Okay. I'll tell you."

And she did. She gave Spur every piece of information that he needed. Some of the towns she mentioned had indeed been hit with bank robberies. After he'd deciphered Buxton's map he could put the two thieves' trails together and, hopefully, solve most or all of the robberies.

Spur left Kitty in the bank and strode to the telegraph office. It was open. One-Eyed Jack grunted to him as the Secret Service agent walked in.

"I know, I know," he said, chewing on his moustache. "The lines are finally up. Seems a buzzard chewed through them or something."

"Just in time."

The telegraph operator grabbed a pencil. "Okay. What's the message?"

"To General Halleck, Washington, D.C. I've put the baby to sleep. We'll be going to Yuma to visit relatives. Fred Hardwick is out of town—again. I watched him leave yesterday. The trouble should be over. Turk, Deadridge, Arizona territory."

One-Eyed Jack busily scratched his words onto a tablet. "That it?" he asked, cocking his head and training his one good eye on his customer.

"Yep."

"Mighty strange message you've got there." He scratched his forehead and looked up at McCoy. "You some kind of lawman or something?"

Spur flipped him a dollar. "Keep the change," he said, and walked out.

On his way back to the Deluxe Hotel for a well deserved breakfast, Spur spotted a familiar face on the street. The bulky Indian man stood on a corner chewing on a piece of straw. He hadn't noticed McCoy, so he slipped up to him.

Spur grabbed the man's arms and twisted them behind his back. "You used to work for Fred Hardwick, didn't you?"

"No. No! That was my brother!"

"Nice try. You nearly strangled me the other day!" He pulled harder.

"Please!" the Indian said in a heavily accented voice. "Don't break my arms!"

"Then talk!"

"Okay. I help Hardwick. White-face pay me money for whiskey. I put rope around your neck. That is all."

"Yeah?"

"Yes! It is truth!"

"Hardwick's dead," Spur said. "I killed him. He murdered two people outside of town."

"I am sorry. I know nothing!"

Spur thought for a moment and released his arms. The Indian spun to face him, rubbing his biceps.

"You almost pull them off!" he said.

"You almost killed me."

The two men looked at each other. The brown-faced Indian's eyes were wary. McCoy finally nodded.

"I could have you arrested for assaulting an agent of the United States Government."

"No!" he said. "I just make money for whiskey!"

"Turtlehead!" a woman's voice called.

The man winced. "Please. My wife!"

"Turtlehead! We go!"

A round woman walked up to them.

She dismissed Spur with a glance. "No talk now. Eat now! Children hungry. You cook food for their bellies!"

McCoy smiled. The woman grabbed Turtleneck's ear and hauled him down the street, screeching at him.

Spur had his breakfast. He did damage to the platters of crisp bacon, endless eggs, biscuits and cups of rich black coffee.

As he ate, McCoy thought of what was ahead. Taking Burt Buxton and Kitty Carson to Yuma. Spending several weeks following Buxton's map, digging up the money he'd buried, then taking it all back to Yuma.

Annemarie Carson stepped into the dining room and flashed him a smile.

It was a dirty job, he thought, but someone had to do it.